THE WITHERING STORM

THE WITHERING MYSTERIES BOOK 3

AMY BOYLES

1

"Grim?" said the man who stood in front of me. He was small, thin in the shoulders and much older than me, probably midsixties. He wore a dark cape over his suit, and when he quirked one of his peppered brows, waiting for an answer to his question, a sparkle twinkled in his eyes.

Or something like that.

Description isn't my thing.

But even if I hadn't immediately recognized the man from the countless television episodes that he'd hosted, the camera crew standing behind him would've instantly tipped me off to his identity.

"Horatio Crooks?" I asked.

He beamed, and that twinkle in his eyes became a shining star. "Horatio Crooks at your service." He gave a half bow. "You wouldn't happen to be Grim, would you?"

"I would be."

"Perfect." He glanced behind him at his crew, and the man holding the camera straightened, ready for action. Horatio turned back to me. "Your uncle says you've been infected by a withering. I'm here to help."

Uncle Geezer clapped a hand on my shoulder. "See? I told you that I knew the old bird. How've you been, Horatio? Gallivanting around the world, searching for monsters, no doubt?"

Horatio turned those sparkling eyes toward my uncle and shook his hand. "Great to see you, Geezer. I didn't think you were still alive after that *whatsiblastit* destroyed your house twenty years ago. Those creatures can truly be devils."

Geezer smiled bashfully. "Oh, you know. When you've seen one *whatsiblastit*, you've seen them all."

My sister, Shelby, shot me a look that said, *What's a* whatsiblastit?

I shrugged as Horatio and his crew of merry cameramen trickled into the house. "Is it okay if we set up here?" The television star twirled around. "This room has great light."

"Of course," Geezer replied with a lopsided grin. "Set up wherever you like. My home is your home."

"Except it's *my* home," my sister said.

"Oh, so it is," my uncle replied with a baffled expression.

Horatio took in my sister's dark shroud of a personality. Perhaps it was the stony look in her eyes. Or maybe it was the fact that her arms were folded. Either way, he turned his full attention to her and said with the utmost humility, "My dear woman. I'm Horatio Crooks, television star of the hit show *Expedition: Monster.*"

"I know who you are."

"So do I." Matt approached, hand out. "I'm a huge fan. I've been watching your show forever. The one episode where you tracked the werewolf to his den and then only had a flaming torch to defend yourself with, was my favorite."

Horatio rocked back on his heels as if he were in a pub about to relay the tale to a roomful of voracious listeners. "Ah,

THE WITHERING STORM

yes, episode 325, 'Inside the Lair of the Beast.' Do you know that none of that was rehearsed? We'd been on the trail of the creature for days, and honestly I was just about to give up. But when we found the cave, I knew we had our man—or beast, as it was. So we went in"—he placed a finger to his mouth and dropped his voice to a whisper—"and I knew this could be the end of me. I said to my crew, 'If you don't want to go, I understand. Men, this is the deadliest challenge we've faced yet.' But they insisted, and so we forged ahead. We'd been at the search for days. Our food was gone, and I was spent magically because I was so tired and hungry. Night was on us, and all we had were the torches. There was a chance that I wouldn't make it out alive. But we went in anyway."

Matt was leaning forward, hinged on every word that came out of Horatio's mouth. "And the way that you defeated the werewolf was classic—with a binding spell!"

Horatio rubbed his chin. "It came to me at the last minute. I said to myself, how can I defeat this creature? What can I possibly cast that will save me and my crew?"

"And you did it," Matt said triumphantly.

"Well, I don't like to take all the credit. It takes a village, you know."

"Horatio, you must be tired from traveling," Geezer interrupted. "Shelby'll make you some tea or coffee for all of you. Whichever you'd like."

"I will?" she said.

Matt shot her a quick look. "I'll help."

"Me too." Paige appeared beside me and grinned up at me. "Let me take your bag, Grim."

The bag that I had packed because I was on my way out of the house—or had been until Horatio arrived. Before I could protest, she snatched the duffel from my hand. "Why don't you sit down and get to know your sister's guests?"

"I was leaving," I grumbled.

"Don't talk nonsense." Geezer steered me toward an empty chair. "Horatio's come all this way to see you. You can't leave now." He deposited me in a chair and scratched his head. "Where'd you say that you were at before this?"

Horatio unbuttoned his cloak and let it slip from his shoulders. With a snap of his fingers, the cloth lifted into the air and hitched itself on a coatrack.

"I was in Fiji tracking a particularly elusive water spirit. But as soon as I heard about the withering, I had to come. Like I told your uncle, Grim, I may be able to help."

I glanced around the room, and my gaze landed on Paige, who was walking off to help with the coffee. She glanced over her shoulder at me and waved her hand toward Horatio, silently telling me to pay attention and not to be so, well, *grim*.

As the crew began taking seats, Geezer mumbled, "We need more chairs."

Next thing I knew, he'd magicked up several more recliners for the men, filling the living room with so many chairs that it resembled a minefield more than a room to relax in.

As soon as he was seated, Horatio fixed his attention on me. "Tell me what happened."

All I wanted to do was leave and find a cure on my own, by myself, away from all this attention. The last thing I wanted to do was spill my guts to a television star.

But Geezer had called Horatio here, so the least I could do was hear him out.

"It started—"

"Hold on." He snapped. "We need to be rolling."

Two cameramen jumped to attention. Lights flared to life, and people were up, working.

"There, that's better. Now, Grim, tell me everything."

"Not on camera."

THE WITHERING STORM

Horatio's eyes flared in surprise. "But, my good man, the world needs to know your story. They need to know what happened to you so that the past won't repeat itself."

"Not. On. Camera," I growled.

He glanced back at the cameramen and gestured for them to lower their instruments. "However you'd like it. But tell me what happened."

When the camera was put away and was no longer a threat, I began. "I made the mistake of taking a withering on. The creature touched me, and I became infected. So here we are."

"Fascinating." He nodded as if I'd told him a ten-minute epic instead of a five-second tale. "Truly fascinating. And what happened to that creature?"

"He was sucked into a book. Where he's to stay," I replied, eyes flashing in warning.

If Horatio thought for one second that I was going to release the creature that had infected me, he was sorely mistaken.

"I understand. Keep the creature where he is. It's best for the world. What an amazing story. Truly fascinating. Tell me" —he leaned in—"I've heard that when one's infected, they begin to feel the *call* of the withering, for lack of a better word. Is that true?"

How did he know that? My face must've betrayed what I was thinking, because a self-satisfied smile ghosted across his face. "Yes, that's what I thought. So it's true then, you begin to associate yourself with the creatures. Have they appeared to you yet?"

Now he knew way too much.

When I didn't answer, he sat back and smirked. "So they are."

"Grim likes to keep his secrets," Geezer said.

"Here we are, back with coffee," Paige announced, placing a steaming cup in front of Horatio.

But he didn't look at the coffee. He stared at me, and I stared back at him. When I was a child, I'd looked up to Horatio as one of my heroes. He was a real monster hunter, someone who helped people. My father had also been a monster hunter, and that was what I'd wanted to be, too. I wanted to help people.

But as I grew older, I started to question his television show, even question Horatio. His series was full of theatrics, but there was very little substance anymore. So I doubted that he'd be able to help me.

But as our gazes locked, his eyes sparking with what I could only assume was hidden knowledge, it hit me that Horatio Crooks might just be the one person on the entire planet who could offer help.

After all, he'd spent an entire lifetime traveling the world, studying just about every monster that existed. He knew more than me about beasts, I'd give him that.

So maybe, just maybe, he knew of a way for me to beat this infection.

Even now, my stomach ached. The transition was beyond painful. Waves of pain overtook me every few moments, waves that I could bite back now. But soon my body would succumb to the agony as it became more excruciating.

Horatio Crooks might just be the one shot I had at salvation.

"How do you know so much about witherings?"

He lifted a hand that was bejeweled with a large ruby ring on the pinky. His crew immediately stopped talking, and my family, along with Paige and Matt, watched the television star in awe.

"May Grim and I have a few minutes of privacy?"

The crew rose, as did Geezer, who stretched his long limbs. "Come on, everyone. I'll take you to the library. We can have coffee in there. But be sure not to ruffle any feathers. The books can be a bit persnickety."

"You can say that again," Shelby said with an eye roll, referencing the last time that we'd been in the library and had narrowly escaped being attacked by the books.

Matt's gaze darted from me to Horatio and back. "Shout if you need anything," he said before falling into the line of folks leaving the room.

Even Savage, my dog, tucked his tail between his legs as he padded out. Paige shot me a smile and brushed her hand over my shoulders before disappearing into the hallway.

Horatio watched as Paige left. As soon as she was gone, he waved his hand, and pressure filled the room. He'd put a silence spell on us.

"Must be a good story, whatever it is you're going to say."

He settled back into his chair and crossed one leg over the other. "Grim, I've spent a lifetime scouring this world for monsters. I've destroyed many, saving the lives of hundreds of thousands of people. If many of the creatures I've encountered had been left to live, they would have wreaked chaos and destruction. The shock wave of hurt left in their wake would have affected more than merely those who were killed at their hand. I've done a service to this world and will leave a legacy that I'm proud of. Few can claim to have done more for humankind."

Truly his ego needed no help in this conversation. "What does that have to do with me?"

"How do I know so much about witherings? The one creature that's the most elusive and yet the most destructive when encountered?"

"It's a question that crossed my mind."

He inhaled sharply. "First swear your secrecy."

Oh, so we were going there, were we? "Why should I?"

"Because what I'm going to tell you will not only change

7

your perception about me, it will change your perception about the very creature that you're becoming."

Well, when he put it that way... "What you say here won't be repeated by me."

"Good." He gave a hard nod. "I know so much about witherings because I was once in your exact same situation."

2

$\mathcal{J}$ waited for Horatio to continue. He paused, eyeing me expectantly, clearly wanting me to ask my next question. "What do you mean, you've been where I am?"

"My dear man, do you really think that in all my journeys, with all the beasts that I've encountered, that I've managed to remain unscathed?"

Well yes, I had. His television show was mostly staged. No company would put their star in mortal danger. But Horatio didn't wait for me to answer, which was good because he wouldn't have liked my thoughts on the subject.

"I have nearly been bitten by werewolves, drained by feral vampires and had my soul sucked from me. I've met every kind of creature on this planet, including your withering. Is it so difficult to think that I may have met your creature and been infected by one?"

"You were infected?"

He nodded. "Mm hm."

"And you're not anymore."

He uncuffed his shirtsleeve and rolled it to his elbow. "I bet your arm is starting to scale, or wither, isn't it? Mine was, too. It's one of the signs of infection. You see where there's a scar?"

A faint silvery line ran from his inner elbow to his wrist. "I see it."

"That's the remnants of what happened to me. But as you can see, I'm cured."

"Tell me everything."

He smirked, looking satisfied that he had my attention. "This happened before I ever got my show. I was a monster hunter back then, too, and a good one. I was finishing a job helping a town capture a water monster that was feeding on the local livestock. I'd destroyed the creature and was leaving. Since I needed to be somewhere early the next day, I left in the middle of the night."

"When more creatures are out," I murmured.

"Granted, it wasn't the wisest choice. I know that now. But like I said, I was in a hurry, and I'd spent so much energy fighting the water creature that I didn't have the power to portal out. So I left in a small rented car. I was maybe two miles from town when I saw the thing. It walked right out onto the road, turned toward me and paused, but then kept right on. I can't tell you the terror that filled my heart."

He pulled a handkerchief from his pocket and blotted his face. "I still break out into a sweat when I think about it." He slipped the cloth into his pocket and sipped his coffee before sighing and settling back into the chair. "I knew what it was right off the bat, of course. I'd read about witherings, but you know as well as I do that it's rare to encounter one. And this one was heading in the direction of the town that I'd just left. So I could keep going and pretend that I hadn't seen it, or stop the creature before it could hurt anyone."

"It wasn't much of a choice, was it?"

"No." He shook his head. "Not after I'd just spent a week with those people. I couldn't let any of them die, so I went in

THE WITHERING STORM

with a headful of steam and the sense that most nineteen-year-olds have, which is to say very little."

I smirked. I remembered being a young monster hunter. You think that you can take anything on. *Anything.* But we're mortal just like all men.

"I parked the vehicle and got out, confronted the beast," he continued. "The encounter didn't last long. I threw everything I had at it, and nothing stopped it. I thought that I almost had it when I enclosed the creature in fire. But even that didn't leave a scratch. It reached through the flames, grabbed me by the throat and touched me here with one long finger." He pointed to the center of his chest.

"That's where I was touched, too."

"So, the same," he said. "Then the withering dropped me and walked back the way that it had come, leaving me, for better or worse, for dead." Horatio sighed and rubbed his face. "I remembered thinking that I'd saved the town. The creature wasn't heading toward them anymore. But when I looked at the spot where his finger had been, there was a mark."

"I have it now."

"Of course you do, or else we wouldn't be here. But I digress. I realized that I was infected with something, so I rushed back to my mentor and told him what had happened. He was horrified. And worse, he said that he couldn't help me."

I quirked a brow. "Then how'd you—"

He lifted his hand to interrupt me. "I'm getting to that. When I realized that he didn't have the power to heal me, there was no choice but to find someone who did. He told me of a well-known wizard who lived halfway across the world, one who was known as a master potion maker. Perhaps he could help. I went to him, but he didn't know what to do, either. Yet he told me about someone else who might have the knowledge that I sought."

His story sounded familiar. I'd gone to my old friend Aaron Strickland to see if he could help. He gave me a journal that only led me to a dead end.

"And on it went," Horatio continued, "until I was sent to an old witch woman who lived deep in the swamps of Louisiana. I can tell by the look on your face that you're skeptical. I was, too. And weeks had passed at this point. The dreams had begun. You know the ones I'm talking about."

I did. Dreams where I was surrounded by witherings who tried to seduce me into the desire to kill. That desire was a pulse that swelled and dipped. Right now the tug was in the back of my mind; it wasn't overpowering—not yet.

"I know the dreams you mean," I told him.

He nodded curtly. There was no reason to dive into them. We both knew how horrific they could be. "Now, I had no faith in this woman. How could a swamp witch help me when even the best healers in the world were stumped on what to do? But she was my last hope. I was turning quickly at this point and realized that if something didn't happen soon, I'd be lost. So I begged for her help, and she gave it. She cured me in stages, giving me a concoction that no one else had. And it wasn't a fast heal. It took weeks for me to overcome my infection. But during that time I stayed with the woman, in one of her beds, and slowly recovered."

Was this too good to be true? Not in all my readings had I come across a cure for a withering infection. To be infected meant doom.

"You were healed."

"Yes."

"And it took weeks."

"Like I said, it wasn't a fast process." Horatio sipped his coffee, staring at me over the rim. "It wasn't over in an instant. I had to go through worse pain than what you're experiencing

THE WITHERING STORM

now in order to come out the other side. But I did it. You can do it, too. With my help."

A television star, a man linked to one of the vainest professions on earth, wanted to help me? What was in it for him?

"You want to film it," I said flatly.

He grimaced. "I prefer to use the word 'record.' But yes, I want to record this transformation. However"—he added quickly—"I also want to record how you're healed. I want all of it."

"No."

"Grim—may I call you that?" I grunted a reply, but he didn't notice. "This isn't just for me and my own selfish needs. We'll be recording you to show the world that not only do witherings exist, but that they pose a dire threat to anyone who encounters one. Plenty of our kind don't even think they exist anymore. They think of witherings as a fairy tale—a grim one. No pun intended."

I was certain it was.

"What you'll be doing is helping others. While I help you." He sat back in the chair and eyed me expectantly. "So. What do you say?"

"No."

His expression fell. "No? Just like that? You won't let me heal you when I have the means?"

"I won't be made into a spectacle. I don't want my life on display for the world to watch."

"And what about those you love? You just want to become a withering, a creature that could return to this house, to places that you remember, and destroy those people?"

"I wouldn't—"

"Wouldn't you?" His jaw flexed in frustration. "How do you know that you wouldn't? You'll remember everything when you become one. I was farther along than you are now when I was healed, and I recall it all. That's why they want you, you know. Because of your connection to people. Because they hate people and want to destroy them. There aren't enough witherings to do that, though, and I get the feeling that those people who turn, many of them end their lives before they become a creature who will destroy their loved ones."

This conversation was growing tedious, so I rubbed my hands down my thighs to help keep my patience reined in. "I was leaving when you arrived. I wasn't going to stay here and harm anyone."

"Ah, but how do you know that you'd stay away? That you wouldn't return? The pull to destroy is very, very powerful."

As much as I hated to admit it, he was right. How did I know that I wouldn't harm those I cared about? What if I left, only to return?

"If you're with me, your loved ones will be safe," he assured me. "Just think, a few weeks with me and you'll be healed. This nightmare will be over."

"And you'll have new viewers."

He hooked a finger in his collar and tugged it down. "Yes, well, it's hard to retain the same audience after twenty years. You must always be replenishing them. You help me do that, Grim, and once this ordeal is over, you'll be a star."

"I don't want to be a star."

"Then take the money that you make from your newfound celebrity, buy an island and retire there. It doesn't matter to me what you do after. But if you want to live, then you must come with me. Otherwise I'm afraid—and I didn't want to bring this up—but I'm afraid that I'll have no choice but to report your answer to the council. I believe you know Carrington Dorn. Is that right?"

I glared at him. Carrington Dorn had made it perfectly clear the last time we met that he planned to keep watch on me. He knew that I was changing, and he wanted to destroy me himself.

THE WITHERING STORM

"How do you know about Carrington?"

He smiled tenderly. "I have friends all over. You can't keep a wizard infected by a withering a secret for very long. People find out. People who will hunt you down if you're not cured. If I were you, I'd rather take my chances with a television star and help boost some ratings instead of being dragged before the council, seen as a threat to society and put down like a dog. Wouldn't you?"

He had me. There wasn't a response I could make that would counter that.

Plus, it was possible that *if* I turned, I'd hunt down my friends and family to destroy them.

Though right now I had a stranglehold on the urge to harm anyone, as the infection penetrated deeper, that same hold couldn't be guaranteed.

He must've sensed my hesitation, because like a lion, Horatio pounced. "You'll come with me, to my house. That's where we'll film, and that's where your treatments will take place. You may bring people with you. I don't expect you to do this alone. But I do expect you to agree to ALL my conditions —which includes being filmed. What do you say?"

I squeezed the armrests of the chair, thinking it over. Stay or go? Die or live?

There wasn't a choice to be made.

"When do we leave?"

3

"*I*'m going with you."

I kicked my bag toward the wall, shoving it out of the way of Horatio's cameramen, who were drifting aimlessly through the living room, looking for something to do. "No, you're not."

Paige placed her fisted hands defiantly on each of her hips. Then she tipped up her chin and narrowed her eyes. "Yes. I. Am. Grim, you're not going away with this man and disappearing on me."

"I was going to disappear on you five minutes ago."

"Well, that's before you decided to head to this Horatio's house to be cured." Her bangs dropped into her eyes, and she blew them away with a perturbed huff. "That was when you didn't know where you were going, but now you do. And I'm coming along."

Several of Horatio's men walked toward us on their way to the door. I pulled Paige out of their path and into the kitchen for privacy. "What will you do there? This cure—it will probably get worse before it gets better. You're not going to like it, and I don't want you to see me that way."

THE WITHERING STORM

"You're afraid? Is that it? You're afraid that I'll see something that'll scare me and I won't care about you anymore?" She cupped her hand to the scruff of my cheek, peering up at me with eyes so full of sorrow that my chest squeezed my lungs to the point of crushing them. "Grim, if you go with him and I never see you again, I wouldn't forgive myself. I was willing to let you leave before Horatio arrived. But now there's a real chance that you'll be cured. Let me come. Let me do this. Let me be there for you."

Her hand slid from my cheek. I snatched it up and placed it over my heart. "You'll serve me better here."

She scoffed and was about to say something when we were interrupted by someone clearing their throat.

Matt rounded the corner and dropped his shoulder to the wall. "She's got a point, Grim. If we're there with you, at Horatio's, it might help you heal faster. You know, we'll be sending good vibes and all that."

I glared at him. "This isn't up for discussion."

"Is my little brother throwing a temper tantrum because he isn't getting his way?" Shelby said as she appeared beside Matt. "Wants to carry his burden alone, is that it?"

I rolled my eyes. "That has nothing to do with it. Where I'm going—"

"Is so cushy that you don't want anyone else to enjoy it?" my sister asked.

"I could die."

"And you could be cured. And best of all," she said, pulling a kitchen towel from her shoulder and smacking me with it as she passed by, "you could be cured with your friends there for moral support. Look, you're going to leave and be on a television show, having all this attention on you—something I know you hate. Why not at least be surrounded by people who care about you?"

Why was it so hard for them to let me do this alone?

Maybe the better question was why I wanted to do it alone.

"I'm trying to keep you safe," I growled at Paige.

"And I will be," she argued. "It's not like Horatio's going to let you harm us. He's not going to risk his own life. I'll be safe."

"Yeah, so will I," Matt added, clapping me on the back. "I've got my things packed. I'm ready to roll when you are."

"You're not goi— none of you are coming with me," I growled.

Horatio stepped into the kitchen. "Are you ready, Grim? The camera crew's already gone ahead. It'll only take a moment to portal to my home, where we can begin your treatments."

I stared at Paige for a long moment as she gave me a hopeful look that speared my heart. I ripped my gaze away.

Before Horatio appeared, I didn't know where I was going or how I'd be healed. Before, it made sense for Paige to remain here. She wasn't safe with me. But wasn't she safe now?

Shelby had a point—Horatio wouldn't allow himself to be harmed. There would be some sort of security, or at least a way to keep me from hurting anyone.

I sighed and pinched the bridge of my nose. "Is it okay if a couple of people come with me?"

"Of course." Horatio clapped his hands. "The more, the merrier. Who's coming?"

"I am." Paige shot me a wide grin. "I'm going with him."

"Me too," Matt said. "I'm Grim's emotional support human."

Good grief. I cocked my head at Shelby. "What about you?"

"What about me? I'm staying here. Someone has to look after Geezer and your dog."

"Thank you." We already had enough people. We didn't need any more.

"That doesn't mean I won't show up later," she replied, looking way too cheerful.

"Are we ready?" Horatio asked, clapping his hands.

Paige winked at me slyly. "I just need to pack a bag. Give me five minutes."

FIVE MINUTES later the four of us—Horatio, Matt, Paige and I—stood in front of a portal. Fog swirled inside the circle, making it impossible to see into the other side.

Paige leaned over. "Is this safe?"

"Perfectly safe," Horatio assured us. "The fog will disappear as soon as we arrive. I keep it so that monsters can't track my home. You can imagine that I have a world of enemies—monsters who'd love to track me down and destroy me. So we keep the fog going year-round. Don't worry, once you get past the gray, the grounds are beautiful. But this will be your first leap of faith in trusting me." He took a good look at the three of us. "Now then, who wants to go first?"

"I will." Matt stepped forward. "I'll make sure the way is safe for all of you."

It took all my strength not to roll my eyes. "How admirable of you."

Matt half bowed. "You know what your problem is, Grim?"

"Just go," I growled.

Horatio gestured for him to enter, and Matt stepped through, disappearing into the mist.

Paige stepped forward, and I grabbed her wrist, stopping her. She shot me a confused look, but I nodded to the portal. I wanted to give it one more second before anyone else went through. Just to make sure the way was safe.

"It's all clear," Matt called from the other side. "Wow. It's beautiful here."

"Convinced it's okay?" she muttered.

"Now I am."

AMY BOYLES

I released her and Paige walked through.

"Only you're left," Horatio told me. "Take this leap of faith, Grim. Trust that I'll be able to do what I say."

I forced back my shoulders and stepped through the portal and into the fog.

The thick gray wall seemed to cling to my skin as I pushed past it and into a clearing. Before me, a lawn filled with lush green grass led up to a hill. On the hill sat a large white house with tall windows. The sound of water came from beyond the home.

As I scanned the horizon, I realized that we were on the edge of a cliff.

Horatio appeared beside me. "The ocean's just beyond the house. I built my home up here, away from prying eyes, though there's a town just down the way. This area is registered as protected land."

"Yet you live here?"

Horatio shrugged. "It pays to be a television star. Come on. Let me give you the grand tour."

By the time I reached the house, Matt was sitting on a deck chair with a white towel draped over his eyes and popping grapes into his mouth.

"Grim, is that you?"

"It's me."

"You've gotta eat these grapes and get a hot towel for your face. You wouldn't believe how refreshing it feels." He thumbed toward a woman standing beside him. "She'll get you whatever you want."

"My name's Drea." The woman offered her hand, palm down, as if she expected me to kiss the back of it.

"This is my daughter," Horatio said. "Drea, meet Grim. We're going to be helping him."

Drea smiled kindly. "I'm glad we're able to help you."

She looked to be in her early thirties and wore dark framed

THE WITHERING STORM

glasses and had her hair pulled back. She kept her head ducked down as if she didn't want anyone to notice her.

For some reason a wave of compassion flowed over me. "Nice to meet you, Drea." The chairs beside Matt were empty. "Where's Paige?"

"She went in to freshen up," Drea explained.

"She had to use the bathroom," Matt added.

"Shall we go inside?" Horatio asked. "Give you the tour?"

"Yes." As I followed him, Matt didn't make a move to enter, so I kicked his foot. "Come on."

"But I'm so comfortable."

"You can get comfortable later."

He grumbled something unintelligible before yanking the towel from his eyes and handing it to Horatio's daughter.

We stepped through a glass sliding door and into a kitchen that was just as white as the outside of the house. Big modern appliances had been installed, and the place was spotless as if no one had ever cooked there.

"I'm here," Paige said, appearing from the hallway. She waved and grinned. "Wow, is this place huge or what? I got lost just going to the bathroom."

Horatio unclasped his cloak, and Drea ran up to slide it from his shoulders and whisk it away to a closet. "It is large. Come, I'm just now giving a tour. This, as you can see, is the kitchen. You're welcome to anything in the refrigerator or to even cook yourself. Mi casa es su casa, as the Italians say. This way, you'll find the living room."

The kitchen opened up to a grand living room that was full —and when I say full, I mean full—of Horatio's kills, both animals and monsters.

Matt crossed his arms. "Is that a brown bear next to a hydra?"

"Baby hydra," Horatio explained, crossing to the creature and patting its head. "This one almost took out my entire

21

crew. These six heads may look harmless now, but they're made to be the most lethal of weapons."

"They don't look that harmless," Paige whispered to me.

She was right. Each of the six had eyes and mouths open, baring daggerlike teeth that looked ready to rip off a chunk of flesh—mine or anyone else's.

"I did the world a favor by taking this creature out. As you look around, there are plaques on each of the creatures, describing what it is. Feel free to ask any questions about monsters you don't recognize."

I knew all of them. There were six not so mythological beasts mingled in with trophy mammals. It was a strange collection.

When we reached a hallway, Horatio pointed to the right. "That way leads to the den. Grim, I'll be meeting you there with my camera crew in about an hour for your first interview. Beyond the den you'll find a sunroom, which leads outside. You're welcome to explore the grounds, but do be careful near the cliff. The edge is solid, but on a few occasions the earth has crumbled away. My suggestion is that you don't get too close to the edge."

He eyed each of us in turn to make sure his words had sunk in. When I nodded, he continued. "Upstairs, you'll find bedrooms. Drea will show you to those. I will see you, Grim, in an hour."

With that Horatio excused himself and headed toward the den. Drea started up the steps, glancing back at us every few seconds.

"Come. Let me show you to your rooms. You're going to love them."

4

ove was certainly not a word I would have used to describe how I felt about my room. Nearly every square inch of wall was covered in black boxes that displayed small winged creatures.

And I wasn't talking about butterflies. These were species that Horatio had perhaps captured and had dried—small sprites, tiny fairies with their wings poked into place. These creatures had faces. Butterflies didn't have faces.

It hurt for me to work any magic, but I wasn't going to sleep with hundreds of glittering eyes glaring at me in accusation every night. I threw up a glamour, hiding them from view.

Someone knocked on the open door as I sat on the bed, testing the mattress. Firm. Good.

"Can I come in?"

Paige stood on the threshold, pushing her shoed toe into the carpet and smiling shyly. "Of course," I told her.

She eyed the walls hungrily. "I like your room. Nice and plain. Mine's covered in posters of monster anatomy. It's like being in a macabre doctor's office."

"Mine's actually worse than that." She lifted an eyebrow and I explained, "I hid the specimens."

"Oh, you get full-on specimens? I'm jealous."

I smiled. She shot me a shy grin and sat beside me. "This bed looks big enough for two."

"Paige," I warned.

"I'm not saying any of that. Just to sleep together. Actually sleep."

"No. I don't trust myself."

"Then maybe you should be chained up."

"Maybe I should be."

Worry flashed in her eyes. "I was joking."

"I wasn't."

We stared at each other for a long moment before she sighed and nodded. "Okay. Got it."

"Got what?"

"That you're building walls even as I'm trying to help you."

I closed my eyes tightly. "I don't want to hurt you."

But you will, said a voice inside my head. *You know you will.*

Get out, I shouted inwardly. That seemed to quiet it. I didn't know if the voice was the withering or my own subconscious goading me. Either way, I didn't want it.

"Come on." She rose and held out her hand. "Horatio's probably ready to interview you."

I slid my palm over hers, unable to stop myself from noticing just how small her hand was compared to mine. Every touch that we shared made me want to touch more of her. It made it extremely difficult not to take her up on her offer of sleeping in the same bed—just for comfort, I knew. But I'd want more than simple closeness. I'd want all of her, and my restraint was frayed as it was. The withering was beating me down inch by inch.

I rose. "I suppose we shouldn't keep Horatio waiting."

She grinned. "I suppose not."

Horatio's study was an intimate room full of dark wood that smelled of orange polish, and tall leaded windows that looked out over the ocean. Where the rest of the house was modern, all white walls and pale marble surfaces, this room was dark and masculine, smelling of old books and cigar smoke. I sniffed, trying to detect a trace of bourbon, but there wasn't one.

The camera crew was the one outlier in the whole scenario. Light boxes surrounded two chairs that were placed in front of a tall fireplace. No one had built a fire. I was grateful for that. My body was already hot enough with the infection. I didn't need any more heat.

But Horatio probably already knew that.

He was sitting in a sleek leather wingback chair, talking to his daughter in hushed whispers when I entered with Paige. Where Horatio was dressed in a manner befitting a celebrity monster hunter—a crisp white shirt with a ruby brooch secured at the collar—his daughter wore overalls and looked like a farmer instead of a celebrity's daughter.

She also wore her hair in pigtails. She must've been late twenties, early thirties, so she clearly wasn't wearing her hair like that for fashion.

She was an odd duck.

When Paige and I entered, Horatio glanced up and rose quickly, striding over with Drea at his heels. "Grim, we're just about ready. Is there anything we can get you?"

"No, I'm fine."

"Wonderful." With military precision, he turned his attention to Paige. "Thank you for escorting him down, but I'm afraid this interview is closed."

"Oh," she said, looking hurt.

Horatio grimaced. "Yes, you see, I want to make sure that

AMY BOYLES

Grim doesn't hold back when he answers any questions. Having friends and loved ones on the set will only impede his possible answers. We're trying to save his life, after all. We can't do that if he keeps anything from us. Which he might do to spare you or anyone else from being hurt."

"Well, sure. I understand." She gave me a big, encouraging smile. "Come find me when you're through."

"Will do."

"I'll follow you out," Drea said, scurrying away like she'd just been caught smoking behind the bleachers of the middle school.

Horatio turned his thousand-watt smile on me. "Ready?"

"Yes." *Let's just get this over with.* "I'm ready."

He motioned for me to take the chair across from him. After the crew checked the lighting, we were ready to roll.

Horatio leaned in. "Grim, just be yourself. We'll be following you throughout this entire process, some of which I'll explain during the interview. The entire world will be watching you, rooting for you, wanting you to get well. Remember that. You have the entire planet on your side."

Right. An entire planet of monster haters. Once they realize I'm becoming what they despise, will they hate me or cheer for me to survive?

"Also, this will be live. We'll be polling the audience as we go. I'll be receiving the results of those polls and they'll be announced. Got it?"

"What kind of—"

"We're on in ten," someone said.

"Ready, Grim? Put on your biggest smile. It's showtime."

"Wait," I said. "What kind of—"

"There's no time for questions."

Behind us, someone said, "And five, four..."

Horatio smiled for the camera. "Hello there, I'm Horatio

Crooks, monster hunter. Tonight we have a very special guest and episode. So grab your favorite snack, settle into your favorite chair and get ready to have your mind blown."

5

"I want you to meet Grim," Horatio said.

Had we discussed using my real name?

He continued, ignoring my scowl. "Grim is in a situation that most of us will never find ourselves, and you should all be thankful for that. But this isn't my story to tell. Let's hear from the man himself." His gaze snapped from the cameras to me. "Would you like to tell the audience what happened?"

No, I wouldn't. "In my line of work, there are risks."

"And what's your line of work?"

"I'm a monster hunter."

"Yes, I believe my audience is aware of the risks of being a monster hunter. You watch the show."

"I've watched since I was a boy."

"You come from a family of hunters, correct?"

"That's right. I've always seen monsters as something that people need to be protected from." He nodded, silently willing me to continue. "And I've always done my job, until recently, when I was attacked by a creature."

"Part of the job, I'm afraid," he said sadly, tsking and shaking his head. Then, like a light switch being flipped, his

THE WITHERING STORM

pity was gone and Horatio was all sparkling eyes and strong intention. "But this wasn't just any creature, was it?"

The light umbrellas surrounding us were bright, and they kept the heat in, which made the spot, or the point of impact, where I'd been originally infected ache. I pushed back my shoulders to redirect the pain, but it didn't help.

"Grim, the creature?"

"Right. No, it wasn't any creature. This was a withering."

He crossed his arms and nodded. "For those in our audience who are unfamiliar with such a beast, can you tell us a little about it?"

"Not much is known of their kind. But what is known, is that there isn't a way to kill them."

"My, and you encountered such a monster. You must've been scared."

"I'm a hunter. There isn't time for fear."

"I know that too well. We have to run in and get the job done, right? No matter the cost. And you paid the ultimate price that night, didn't you?"

I exhaled heavily. It felt like I was sitting on an examination table in a teaching hospital, surrounded by interns all playing at being doctors.

"The withering touched me, and I was infected."

Horatio gasped. "Infected? With what?"

All this theatre was giving me a headache. "It infected me with itself."

Horatio leaned forward. "What does that mean?"

"It means that I'm slowly becoming one of them."

His head snapped to the camera. "Ladies and gentleman, Grim has been infected by one of the deadliest and most elusive creatures known to us hunters. Some in our profession don't believe in the existence of witherings. But I do. I've seen one before. They are, indeed, nearly impossible to kill, but it can be done."

"What?"

He ignored me. "But Grim, you didn't come to me looking to be put out of your misery. You came to me for another reason. What is that?"

If we were being technical, I didn't come to him at all. "To see if you could help."

"And help you I can. You have two choices here: become the very creature you despise, or you can be cured. The road to being cured is tedious, and it isn't over in a day. But it can be done. I can help you. Isn't that what you want?"

This felt like a setup. "Yes, it's what I want."

He clapped his hands. "Audience, Grim wants to be cured. Is that what you think should happen? Do you want Grim to become a withering, a slow and painful transformation, so that you can see what that monster is? Or would you like for Grim to be cured, to be the human that he's supposed to be?" His gaze flicked to me. "Grim, you may need to show them the infection for them to vote."

Vote?

"Open your shirt and show them."

"No."

His mouth twitched. Not used to being told no, I assumed. "Please."

I rolled my eyes. "Okay."

Then I unbuttoned my shirt and opened it enough for the cameras. I didn't have to look directly at it for the inky blackness to fill my peripheral vision. I knew what it looked like. My skin was ebony where I'd been struck. The circle was growing, with black tentacles reaching for the rest of my skin as it tried to take over my body.

"That looks painful," Horatio murmured.

"It is." I buttoned my shirt and eased back into the chair. "But hopefully I'll be healed soon enough."

"Yes, back to that. Ladies and gentleman, at the bottom of

your screens you'll see two sets of numbers. If you want Grim to become a monster, send a text to that number. If you prefer that he be healed, text to the number that corresponds to that choice. We'll have the results when we come back from this commercial break."

"And we're clear," the director said.

I sat, stunned, staring at Horatio, who was immediately flocked by a makeup person and someone who handed him a cup of water.

He glanced over at me. "Water, Grim?"

"What is going on?" I growled. "What do you mean, they're voting? You said that you'd be polling them, not asking them to vote like this is *America's Got Talent*."

He shrugged. "We're trying a new format, live texting during the show. We want the audience to feel involved, so we're letting them decide your fate."

"What?" I shouted.

"Calm down. It's all rigged. No one's going to let you become a monster. It's just a hook. This is theatre, Grim. We want them to feel like they're a part of the show"—he winked —"even if they're not."

I bit down my rage. "So you're saying that you're letting the audience think that they're deciding my fate."

"Exactly."

"We're back in thirty," the director announced.

Outside the room, voices rose. "I'm going in there! You're not keeping me from him!"

Paige.

The door flew open, and she stormed in, hair flying behind her and with Matt right on her heels.

Fright filled Horatio's face. "Get them out of here."

"What's going on?" Paige demanded, eyes burning with anger. "You're not doing this to Grim."

"No, you're not," Matt added.

"I tried to stop them from coming in," Drea apologized to her father.

"We're back in ten," someone called. "Get them out of here."

"Paige, Matt. It's fine," I said. "This isn't real."

Her expression was frantic. "What do you mean?"

"I'll explain later."

"Get them out," Horatio commanded Drea.

Drea grabbed each of them by the sleeve. "We've got to go."

"I'm not going anywhere," Paige fumed.

"In five," someone called.

Horatio looked like his head was about to explode. There wasn't time for them to leave the room, so I said quickly, "Stand out of the way, against the wall."

Paige nodded hard before grabbing Matt by the sleeve and pulling him to the wall.

"In five, four..."

Horatio watched the trio with a cold expression until he was satisfied that they were safely against the wall and out of view. When the red light flared on the camera, he plastered on his celebrity smile.

"We're back with Grim, a monster hunter, who's been infected with a deadly disease, one that will turn him into a beast, one of the very creatures he's spent his life hunting. I have a cure for this disease, but healing him won't be easy." His gaze darted to me. "It won't be, Grim. You need to know that right now. You may feel like you're dying, like there's no hope. But in order for you to be saved, you must experience the depths of agony. You see"—he fisted his hand—"the hold that the withering has on you goes beneath the surface. Those monsters have a hold on your soul, and that's what we're fighting for—your very soul."

This suddenly became much more dramatic than I'd anticipated.

THE WITHERING STORM

"But don't worry," Horatio quickly added. "As long as the audience believes you should be saved and not left to turn into a monster, we'll deliver your soul from whatever depths the withering wants to drag it down to. You will be freed from this misery. And it is misery, isn't it?"

He'd spoken for so long that when Horatio finally prompted me to talk, it took a minute to form a coherent thought.

"Isn't it misery, Grim?"

"Um, yes. It's misery. Absolutely."

"Tell us about it."

No. "I have urges."

"What sort of urges?" he asked with the gusto of a tiger about to pounce on its prey. I glared at him. Baring my inner thoughts and feelings wasn't part of this arrangement. "This will help the audience decide your fate."

All this talk of the audience made a knot ball up in my stomach. They weren't deciding anything about me. Strangers wouldn't hold my future in their hands.

"Please tell us," he pleaded.

Fine. "Witherings are evil, and not only have they infected me with a disease that will turn me physically into one of them, I'm also feeling the mental strain of their attacks. My thoughts are often dark. Sometimes I want to hurt others, people that I care about and would never normally harm."

"Won't you tell us about that?"

"No, I won't."

Annoyance flickered across his face, but it quickly dissolved. "It will help them—"

"No," I seethed.

I wasn't going to tell him about the urge to place my hands around Paige's neck and squeeze until the life left her. She was standing in the room, and even if she wasn't and would never see this interview, that wasn't information I would share.

"I understand," Horatio replied calmly. "I think our audience knows enough about you and about the situation in order to make an informed voting decision. If you haven't texted your choice to the number on your screen, do so now, because the results are about to be pulled. And while we're tallying those results, I want to give you a look at what the next weeks will look like with Grim. If you choose to let him be healed, you'll witness what that will be, and I can speak from experience that it won't be pretty. Grim will be in pain—more pain than he's in right now. But you can rest assured in the knowledge that he will survive.

"On the other hand, if you decide for him to become the creature that's infected him, I'm afraid our time here will be cut short because Grim will be taken into custody by the council and they'll do with him what they see fit in order to keep the rest of us safe."

My eyes flared. Horatio was going to hand me over? That wouldn't happen. I wouldn't allow it.

"But," he added, his voice pleasant, "I know that all of you will make the right decision. Grim, are you ready to hear the results?"

"Yes," I growled.

"Very well."

Someone to the side handed Horatio a tablet, and he glanced at it, nodding. "Interesting." His head snapped up, and he looked directly into the camera. "I have the results right here. The audience has decided overwhelmingly that they want Grim to be healed! Isn't that wonderful news?" he asked me.

"Yes," I grumbled. "Great."

Horatio grinned. "Come back next time to witness how we're going to heal our very own monster hunter. Until then, be sure to keep those monsters under your bed, where they belong."

THE WITHERING STORM

"And we're clear," someone yelled.

Horatio rose at the same time I did. "Good job, Grim. The audience overwhelming loves you and wants you to be well." He flashed the tablet at me. It was a mess of graphs that I had no interest in deciphering.

"You've directly brought the council into this," I accused.

"Of course I did. Putting you on camera meant that they'd find out."

"I didn't realize we'd be live," I argued.

The doorbell rang and Drea excused herself to answer it. Paige and Matt approached me.

"They've already threatened Grim once," Paige said.

"What are you trying to do, get him killed?" Matt accused.

Horatio patted the air calmly. "Now, now. Let's all settle down. Everything's going to be fi—"

"Carrington Dorn's here," Drea said from the doorway. She dropped her voice. "And he looks mad."

A gigantic smile formed on Horatio's mouth. "Right on time. Come, Grim. Let's find out what our guest wants. No doubt to kill you himself." He winked at me. "Let's see if we can talk him out of it."

6

Carrington Dorn was leaning against a wall when the five of us entered the foyer. He'd been staring at the floor, but when he heard us, his head zipped up and his dark gaze landed on me.

He scowled.

I scowled back.

His white-blond hair was gelled away from his face in thick, crusted ropes. He wore black from head to toe—like any good hunter, or lackey for the council.

He even wore black gloves and it wasn't cold outside.

No doubt to keep any blood off his hands.

"Councilman Dorn, to what do I owe this honor?" Horatio said, the words falling off his tongue thick as molasses.

The scowl on Dorn's face deepened. "You know why I'm here."

"I'm afraid that I don't, but we can discuss it over a glass of wine."

"I'm on duty."

The celebrity's brows lifted. "Water, then?"

THE WITHERING STORM

"No, thank you. I don't want anything. I'm here because you're harboring a dangerous person."

"Who? Grim?" Horatio's gaze washed up and down me. "He doesn't look dangerous to me."

"You have to turn him over to us. He's infected." Here, Dorn turned to me. "I knew you were infected. You couldn't hide it from me."

Before I could answer, Horatio took a step in front of me. Horatio wasn't a big man. I could still see over his head and meet Dorn's glaring eyes.

"You're not taking Grim anywhere, Dorn. You have no authority. Besides, I'm going to heal him. What would the public say if the council took Grim and did whatever it is you're going to do—dispose of him, I suppose? How would the people react to that travesty of justice, especially when they've just voted to see him live?"

Dorn's face, which was already pale, turned white as porcelain. "They'd understand."

"I don't think they would. In a few days I'd have to return to my audience and explain that my home was raided by government officials who took Grim away, never to be seen again."

"You wouldn't say that."

"Oh? You think that I'd lie and tell them that Grim changed his mind? He's infected with a dangerous virus running through his veins, and people are simply going to believe that he opted out of saving himself? The audience isn't that stupid."

"Aren't they?" Dorn sneered. "They'll believe whatever we tell them."

"Then you tell them what you want. I have a permit to keep any kind of creature I choose to, as is my agreement with the council." He opened his palm, and a scroll appeared in his hand. Just as quickly as it appeared, it unrolled, coming to a bouncing halt at his knees. "This agreement says that I'm allowed to keep any beast of my choosing—alive or dead. You see, I'm a responsible member of society. I don't cause harm, and the council lets me do what I want. So you're out of line here, Dorn, which means you can either stay and be friendly, or you can leave."

Dorn leaned in and studied the scroll. As he read it, his face went from pale to red, to more red, to extreme plum.

"It's all regulation," Horatio said as Dorn opened his mouth and was about to, no doubt, argue just about any and every fact that he could on the page. "You've been outdone here, but like I said, you may join us for drinks."

"No, thank you. I don't think that I will. But I will be checking up on you, Horatio, and your little experiment." His eyes flashed on me. "If you really think he can save you, then you're out of your mind."

"Enough," Horatio snapped.

Dorn lifted his hands in surrender. "I'm leaving. Don't worry. I wouldn't stay in this madhouse one minute longer."

With that, he whipped around, coattails flapping, opened the front door by lifting his hand and disappeared as soon as he had crossed the threshold.

There was a moment of silence before Matt broke it. "I get the feeling he wasn't too happy. What do you think?"

Horatio smiled tightly. "We have nothing to worry about with him. He doesn't have jurisdiction here, and he knows it." He flipped up the collar of his shirt. "Come, everyone. Let's have something to drink. I could use a refreshment after that."

Matt raked his fingers through his hair. "I'm with you."

Horatio, Matt and Drea walked toward the kitchen while I still watched the front door, which stood wide open. I closed it and turned around to find Paige staring at me.

She dropped her voice. "Do you think what he said's true? About Horatio not being able to save you?"

"No. Horatio knows what he's doing."

She nodded absently. "But what if he doesn't?"

"Then I'm no worse off than I was before, am I?"

"I guess not." Paige stepped forward, tipped up her face and sighed. "I just want you to be okay."

"I know. I do, too."

She wrapped her arms around my waist and hugged me to her. I closed my eyes, anticipating that violence would overtake me, but for a moment I was at peace. I slipped my arms over her back and squeezed her close, relishing in the scent of her shampoo—strawberries and...something. Female scents weren't my expertise.

But for this one moment my head was clear, and I wanted to enjoy it.

"We'll get through this," she whispered.

I dropped my mouth to the top of her head and kissed her. "One way or another."

"You don't have to say it like that."

"How would you prefer I say it?"

"With hope."

"Ah."

"You can at least pretend to have some."

That made me chuckle. "I have hope."

She tilted back her head and studied me with a look that made a line form between her brows. "Do you really have hope?"

"Of course I do. Come on." I untangled her arms from around me. "Let's get something to drink. I could use water after that interview."

"Okay."

As we walked arm in arm toward the kitchen, guilt tightened in my gut. Of course I didn't have hope. But I couldn't let Paige know that.

7

"We're starting your treatments today," Horatio said the next morning. I was still digesting everything that had happened over the past day—the audience poll and Carrington Dorn appearing, wanting to cage me like a beast.

I didn't see a cage, but he was probably stowing it in his back pocket.

Horatio, Matt, Paige and I sat at the dining table while Drea scurried around waiting on us—pouring orange juice and coffee, dropping a plate of cinnamon rolls in the center of the table, delivering sausages.

Basically she was Horatio's maid.

"Today?" Paige asked, then took a bite of sausage. "That's good." She rubbed my leg. "That's great."

"It is exciting, but there are things you need to know about the treatment."

I sipped my coffee. "What things?"

He placed his fork atop his plate and folded his hands. "First, it will seem like you're getting worse before you get

THE WITHERING STORM

better. I went through the same experience. But you have to trust me. I know what I'm doing."

"Even though you've never done this to someone else?"

He smiled tightly. "The witch gave me specific instructions, and I've got enough medicine to start."

"To start?" Matt said, startled. "What about to finish?"

"We'll need to acquire more."

"From where?" I asked.

Horatio patted the air like he was trying to calm a screaming child. "All things in good time. We'll get to it when we get to it. For now, all you need to know is that we have enough, but that we'll eventually require more."

Horatio glanced at his plate, and from across the table, Matt shot me a concerned look. I nodded slightly, telling him to settle down. We'd come this far. We had to remain on the path.

"But as I said, there are rules," Horatio told us. "The first is that you must trust what I say, and do it. All of it, even if you don't want to, or even if it goes against what you think is the right choice. Do you understand?"

"I understand," Matt said.

Paige kicked him from under the table.

"Ow. Oh." His eyes flared with understanding when she gritted her teeth. "Do you promise to do as Horatio says, Grim?"

When I didn't answer, Horatio's gaze swung to me. "Well, do you?"

"Yes. As long as it doesn't mean your audience has sentenced me to death."

He laughed. "They're not going to do that. They want a good redemption story. We all do. They want to know that you're going to live, and when you do, they'll feel like they were a part of that. They'll be connected to you in ways you can't imagine."

I grunted, not interested in being connected to strangers who watched reality TV.

Drea sat at the other end of the table and started building her plate. Horatio watched her for a moment before saying, "The next rule is that the medicine will make your skin sensitive to the sun, so while you're on it, you can't go outside."

I frowned. "Not at all?"

"I'm afraid not. I wish that weren't the case, but it is. You'll need to stay in the house. But don't worry, we'll find plenty of ways to keep you occupied so that you don't feel as if you're a prisoner."

I doubted it. The windows were tall and wide, letting plenty of sunshine spill into the house, but that was no substitute for feeling the warm sun on your face, drinking in the scent of a cool breeze.

"What's next? We won't be able to feed Grim after midnight?" Matt joked, referencing the movie *Gremlins*.

"Be careful what you wish for," Drea replied, her lips tipped into a hungry smile.

Why was she smiling like that?

"Drea," her father scolded, "you know as well as I do that there's no such rule. Grim may eat whenever he chooses, though he might lose his appetite for a time."

"Is there another rule?" I asked.

He shook his head. "Those are the main ones—do as I say and don't go outside. If others creep up while we're working, then I'll convey them then. But as for now, that's it. So. Are you ready to get started?"

"I am."

"Good." He wiped his napkin over his mouth. "Then we begin after breakfast."

THE WITHERING STORM

AFTER BREAKFAST WAS CLEANED up and the dishes put away, Horatio led us to a wing of the house that I hadn't explored. There was a long hallway that was lined on both sides with glass, which led to more rooms—a den, it looked like, and a bedroom.

We stopped in front of a steel door that was taller than me and twice as wide.

Horatio punched a code into a panel located on the wall, and the distinct *snick* of a bolt unlocking came from the door. Horatio opened it, and lights flickered to life, revealing a steep staircase.

"This is my lab," he told us as we followed him down the steps. "It's where I'll give you the medicine, and also where we'll watch you. If you need observing, that is." He glanced over his shoulder at me. "But I don't think it'll come to that."

The air was distinctly chillier in here than in the rest of the house. In front of me, Paige shivered. I pulled my sweater off and placed it over her shoulders. She shot me a grateful smile.

At the foot of the stairs the subterranean level came into full view. The walls and ceiling were silvery steel, and long tables stretched out over the length of the space. The whole room was smaller than I'd expected, and fairly sparse. It didn't look like Horatio actually worked any experiments down here, so it wasn't clear why he needed a lab.

"I know it's not much," he said as if reading my mind. "But I don't need much room, as I'm mostly out and about, exploring the world, helping those in need."

Matt ran a hand up the back of his head, making the brown strands spike up. "Why would you need a lab at all?"

Horatio ignored him and turned to me. "Grim, I need you to sit here."

Situated at one end of the room was a padded examination table. I didn't understand why he would need one, and it looked out of place among the slick steel surfaces.

"You bring people infected with the withering virus here often?" I joked.

His jaw tensed. "No. But Drea, when she was a child, was prone to getting hurt—sprained ankles, lots of cuts, so I had one installed."

Drea shrugs. "What can I say, I'm accident-prone."

"But you're all better now, aren't you?"

"Me?" Drea nods enthusiastically. "I'm great. Never better. But don't worry, Grim. The table's been sterilized. You won't get any germs—at least not from me."

"That's comforting." I supposed.

Voices sounded from behind us, and I turned to see the camera crew streaming into the room. I scowled as Horatio said, "You don't mind them filming, do you? We have to let the people see what's going on with you, Grim. We're chronicling your experience. After all, as far as we know, no one has ever had this treatment, or even this infection, filmed. You are history in the making, my boy, and the whole world wants to root for you to live."

Not comforting.

I had the feeling that even if I objected to being filmed, Horatio would have them record me one way or another. At this point I was in for a penny. So I might as well be in for a pound.

"It's fine," I told him.

"Good. Men, you can set up over there."

As they did what they were told, Paige asked, her voice shaking from nerves, "Are they just going to pop up every now and then without warning?"

"Oh, I'm warned," the TV star explained, as if that made a difference.

"But we're not," she bit out.

"My dear, this is what needs to be done. You don't want to keep the public from this knowledge, do you? The world needs to know that witherings exist and that they are dangerous creatures. Your boyfriend?" He lifted his brows and she nodded. "Your boyfriend is, in one way or another, saving the world. That should mean something to you. It should mean that you're happy to share this experience with my audience because who knows who else might be helped."

Paige shot me a worried look, and I said, "It's okay."

She held my gaze for several more seconds before nodding. "If you say so."

"Are we all set then?" Horatio asked. When none of us argued, he nodded to the table, and I sat atop it, feeling like this was the strangest examination that I'd ever gone through.

Horatio pulled a buckle from under the bed. "The doses hurt, or else I would never ask this of you. Not only do they hurt, but they can elicit a strange reaction every time you're given what heals you."

My gaze hardened at the restraint in his hand. "You're buckling me down."

"Not only for your safety but for ours. When I was given my first dose, the witch tied me to a tree."

"I thought you couldn't go outside," Paige asked.

Horatio smiled tightly. He did not like to be questioned. "The first dose is okay. But after this one, you will be sequestered to the house. Now, as I was saying, that first dose enraged me. I wanted to harm anyone and everyone. I would've probably killed the witch with my bare hands if she hadn't strapped me to that tree. So. That's why we're doing this. Do you understand and accept these conditions?"

"We're not going anywhere," Paige told me.

I nodded, and Horatio and Drea strapped my arms to the bed.

"Lie back," he instructed. "Get as comfortable as possible. I know it's difficult with the lights, but the cushion is soft."

I did as he said. Horatio nodded to Drea, and she moved to

a glass box, where she placed a finger on a pad that lit up, recognizing her fingerprint, and then a drawer popped open.

"This won't look like a regular pill, because no one has made a pill for what you have," he explained.

"What is it?"

"This is sourced carefully and is the last of its kind."

"But how will we get more for his other treatments?" Paige said, worry lacing her voice. "You said that he'll have to be treated more than once."

"He will." He smiled at her. "We'll get more. Drea and I are working on it."

"But how can you be sure?" she asked, her voice rising.

"Trust, my dear Paige," Horatio said soothingly. "You must trust us if Grim is to be healed."

"We trust you." But her brows were pinched together, suggesting she wasn't completely on board with this.

"It'll be fine," I told her.

She forced herself to smile and took my hand. "Yeah. It'll all be okay."

Horatio cleared his throat. "Water, Drea."

"Oh, right." She poked the air dramatically and scurried over to a community water cooler, dispensing some spring water into a small plastic cup. She hustled back over and handed it to her father. "Here you go."

"Now the cure."

She squeezed her hands into a pair of latex gloves and tweezed the cure from the glass drawer.

"You'll want to take it with water," he instructed, handing me the cup. "Open your hand."

I did as he said, and Drea dropped the cure into my palm. It was most definitely not a pill. If anything, it looked like someone had cut up a kitchen sponge, painted it light brown and stuck it in a drawer.

I didn't like to put foreign objects in my body. "What is it?"

THE WITHERING STORM

"It's a very rare fungus that the witch gave me," he explained. "We've worked on cultivating more."

Matt scratched his head. "Where were you growing it?"

"Behind that door." He pointed to a steel door at the other end of the room. I hadn't noticed it and for good reason. It looked like part of the wall. The only thing that gave its presence away was a handprint panel beside it. "Now. Grim, please take the cure and drink the water. It'll help quell the bitter aftertaste." He turned to the camera crew. "You can begin filming now." When the camera was on, the celebrity said, "Audience, you are about to witness Grim taking the first dose of the cure. Watch carefully. What you're about to witness has never before been recorded."

I looked at my audience, stopping to study Paige, to drink in her beauty—the long brown hair, her big eyes, the easy smile she usually had on her lips.

"Bottom's up."

I popped the fungus into my mouth. Bitter didn't even begin to describe the taste. It tasted like dirt and death mixed in with manure. I tossed back the water, swallowed the thing whole and prepared to bite down on whatever came next.

8

*T*he fungus was as spongy as it looked as it slid down my throat. I swallowed it in one gulp and bit down against the bitterness that overcame me.

"Well?" Horatio asked, eyes wide and sparkling, filled with curiosity. "How do you feel?"

"Fine."

Not a lie. I felt exactly the same.

Until I didn't.

Pain sliced through my gut, and I doubled over.

"Grim!" Paige lunged for me. "Are you okay?"

"Don't touch him." Horatio grabbed her by the arms and held her fast. "Leave him alone. We don't know how he'll react, and I'm not putting anyone's life in danger. If that happens, Carrington Dorn will have a reason to take Grim away."

Her expression fell. "Are you okay?"

Yes. No. "Pain."

"Can you tell us where?" Horatio asked with all the comfort of a scientist asking a test subject if an electric shock hurt them.

THE WITHERING STORM

"Chest," I grunted.

My torso was on fire. It felt like my shirt was melting onto my flesh. It was horrible. Clamping my teeth tight did nothing to stop the agony.

"Drea, open his shirt," Horatio commanded.

"Are you sure?"

"Yes. We must see what's happening. There could be a secondary injury that we'll need to deal with."

Drea took a scalpel from a silver tray. I hoped that thing was sterilized. She approached timidly. "I'm not going to cut you."

A roar ripped from my throat. I couldn't temper the pain, and yelling was the only way to relieve even a fraction of the anguish.

Drea grabbed my shirt and quickly sliced through the fabric.

"Stand back, everyone." Horatio threw open the fabric and everyone gasped.

When I looked down, I understood why. My skin was boiling, bubbling like a cauldron.

"Do not be alarmed," Horatio announced. "Grim is healing. This is the first step in the process. The cure is working. It's fighting the infection. You are in pain now, but it will subside. And you may begin to experience worse."

His words were right on cue. At that moment the voice that had infiltrated my head before, but I'd managed to shove away, came roaring back.

Grim, you can never get rid of me. I will be with you. Even now, you feel the rage burning down in you, don't you? You feel it. You feel the anger, the temptation, the urge to destroy.

Get out of my head, I yelled back.

Look at her. Look at that pretty little thing you love.

My gaze snapped to Paige. Her face was white as paper, her

eyes big as plates. She was scared to death for me, *of me.* I didn't know which.

Wouldn't you just love, the voice continued, *to put your hands around her neck?*

"No," I shouted.

The sound came from deep inside me and ricocheted against the walls, slamming into glass vials lined up on a table.

One by one, the vials shattered, hit by my sonic boom. Everyone covered their ears.

Paige collapsed to the floor. Matt dropped and placed a comforting hand on her back. Drea winced as she clasped her hands tight to the sides of her head. All the while, Horatio just smiled and nodded.

As soon as the scream faded, the agony in my chest subsided. My skin stopped boiling, and everything calmed.

"And cut!" The celebrity star grinned. "You did it, my boy. You survived the first dose of the cure. Do you feel better?"

I did a mental check. The pain in my chest had cooled. When I looked down, the black inky lines that had wrapped around my forearms had shrunk, pulling in toward my torso.

And the voice...it wasn't right on the edges of my mind, ready to sneak past my mental barriers and invade me. Yes, I felt better.

"I do," I confessed.

"Good. Well, you can understand why I wouldn't want to film that for the audience, but we will keep them up to date on your progress. Drea, you may free him."

"Yes, Father."

"What about the second dose?" Paige asked. "When will he get it?"

"Soon. Very soon." He poked the air with a flourish. "Now, Grim. Do you feel strong enough to walk? I know that dose must've taken some of your strength. You look good, by the way, and your skin will continue to heal over the coming days. We'll do another TV episode this week to update the fans on your progress. In the meantime, the crew will be around, here and there. They may film you while you're doing mundane things like eating. Pay them no mind. Act as if they don't exist."

Paige came over and took my hand. When I'd touched her before, the anger had overtaken me, the rage and carnal desires of predator and prey had sunk into my bones. But now I didn't feel any of those. All I wanted was to run my hands through her hair and crush my lips against hers.

"How are you?" she asked.

"Better, though weak."

"Think you can stand?"

"For you? Anything."

I rose and took a step. Surprisingly I felt stronger than I had in days. Whatever this cure was, it worked. I just hoped that Horatio had enough to finish the job.

Horatio beamed at us. "Well, all that curing has given me an appetite. Who wants a snack?"

Matt raised his hand. "Is it wrong to say no?"

TURNED out that everyone was hungry. All that curing gave one an appetite. After a few minutes I was tired of being inside, so I headed for the door in the living room that led off to the backyard.

The view from this room was breathtaking. Large windows faced the ocean and the cliff. The grass unrolled for easily fifty yards before it just stopped, ending at the sky. I wanted, for at least a few brief moments, to experience the outdoors—feel the breeze, enjoy the sunshine on my face until I couldn't anymore.

But as soon as I turned the knob, a voice stopped me. "Where are you going?"

Drea stood with her arms crossed, tapping her foot. She scowled, nodding at my hand, which was still attached to the doorknob.

"I wanted to go outside for a moment."

She shook her head. "No going outside. The sun is bad for you."

"Already?"

"Already."

I lifted my hand in a surrender gesture. "Then I'll stay in here."

"Good."

With that, she turned and left the room. I gazed longingly out the window, wondering how long I'd have to be kept away from the sunlight. Probably until I was through with my treatments. But how long would that be?

"Already trying to break the rules, I see," Horatio announced as he entered the room.

I raked my fingers through my hair. "I didn't realize that the medicine would affect me so quickly."

"Instantaneous," he admitted, slipping his hands into his pockets. "But don't be angry at Drea for telling me. She's only looking out for you. Wants to keep you safe. After all, the ratings from last night were our highest ever."

The camera crew spilled into the living room, and the director said, "We'll head back to the guest house to review the footage."

"Wonderful," Horatio replied as they all streamed out of the room.

When they were gone, I said, "They're staying?"

Surprise flitted across his face. "Well yes, of course. Now that you've taken the first dose of cure, we need to be filming you, to make sure that you're okay, that you're responding in the right way. The viewers, Grim—"

"They'll want to see," I spat. "I know."

His eyes narrowed at my tone. "Don't forget that what you're doing is important for all of mankind. If I could have recorded my own journey, I would have. But I didn't, and I regret it. Of course I wasn't an international superstar at the time. But now that I am, I won't miss an opportunity to make sure that your cure is recorded for the world."

The way he looked at me suggested that Horatio was used to people groveling in thanks. Not going to happen. He was getting just as much out of this relationship as I was. He was enriching himself off increased viewership, and I was keeping my life.

Or so I hoped.

"Why don't you get some rest?" he asked. "I'm sure you're tired."

I was tired. "I could lie down."

"I'll take you up," Paige said, appearing in the room. "Come on."

As we excused ourselves from the living room and Horatio's presence, I had the distinct feeling that he might have been getting even more from this relationship than me.

But how? And more importantly, what?

9

That night I couldn't sleep. After staring at the ceiling for hours, I couldn't lie in bed anymore. I had to get up.

The house was quiet as I made my way into the living room. Moonlight streamed through the windows, splashing in thick sheets onto the floor.

The trees waved in a light breeze, tempting me outside.

After all, Horatio had never said anything about me not being able to go outside at night, did he?

I opened the door and slipped into the darkness.

Cool air blew over my neck and shoulders as I made my way across the grass. I walked to the cliff and looked down at the ocean. I could hear water crashing against the rocks below. It roared in anger, as if it had a personality all its own.

How would I be able to stay indoors for as long as this cure took? And how long *would* it take? Horatio hadn't given a time frame.

Better enjoy this while I could. Because if the celebrity got wind of me being outside, I had a feeling that he'd start locking me in my room at night.

No, he hadn't said that I couldn't roam at night, but he hadn't said that I could, either.

I walked around the house and down the hill, past the fog. A vast expanse of trees lay at the base, and just beyond them sat a small town. Amber light flared off in the distance. The town was perhaps half a mile away, and since I had nothing else to do...I decided to explore.

It had been a long time since I'd walked a town at night looking for monsters. Not that I expected to find any here with Horatio living so close by. My guess was that if there was even a whiff of a creature, the townsfolk would be ringing his bell and begging him to get rid of any unwanted critters.

But still, the idea of ambling about to see what I could find was too tempting to pass by.

The downtown area was locked up tight by the time that I arrived. A few homes were sprinkled along streets outside the main buildings. The town reminded me of one nestled deep in the Rockies, surrounded by mountains. You wouldn't even know the place existed except for stumbling on it.

I walked the abandoned streets, drinking in the quiet and the normalcy. Everything about this town felt safe, secure. Nothing ever happened here. It was the sort of place where people raised children, where they slowed down and where they enjoyed life.

A panting sound came from the shadows, and my hackles rose. I lifted my hand, ready to throw whatever magic I had at the ready. I wasn't at full power, not even close thanks to the infection. But the cure had helped some today, and I felt stronger than I had in a week.

The panting grew louder, and I ignited my magic. Power flared in my palms, and I was about to throw it when a dog padded into view.

He was tall and lanky, looked part hound dog, with long,

floppy ears. He wore a collar and approached with his tongue out, eyes bright.

"What're you doing out here, boy? You should be home."

The dog let me pet him, gave a wag of his tail, and then he was off, trotting down the road on his way to wherever he was going.

I spent another ten minutes walking the streets, looking for...well, anything. I didn't know what I was searching for besides a distraction, any distraction from being locked up in Horatio's house all day.

But all good things come to an end, and this one did when I was heading back.

It started with the rustle of trees. There was a sliver of moonlight, but surrounding the town was a thick tree line, one so thick that I couldn't see through it.

But I could hear through it.

And what I heard was a growl. It was low, guttural, almost sounding like whatever was making it had a mouth full of water.

I stopped walking.

The hairs on the back of my neck straightened. This wasn't the growl of a dog. It wasn't the growl of any normal mammal. This was too loud, too raspy.

I ignited my magic, creating a ball of light that balanced in my palm.

The growling stopped, but only for a moment.

Any normal person would've backed away. They would have turned toward their destination and left.

But that's not how monster hunters think. Instead of retreating from a fire, we dive straight into it.

It's not always the best idea. Even I'll admit that.

I quietly stepped toward the woods, hand lifted, trying to see past the thick foliage. The branches gave when I pushed them away, and the growling began again.

THE WITHERING STORM

Something moved in the darkness. A shadow slipped to my left. The growling intensified, turning into snarls of warning.

I should have stayed back. I should have listened. But I didn't.

The only way to see what was hiding in front of me was to throw my light into the darkness, which could do one of two things—scare whatever was hiding or anger it into attacking.

I was hoping on the former. So I took a deep breath and tossed the orb toward the sounds.

The light landed on the dry leaves lining the tree bed with a *crunch*. Light splashed up, and there stood the creature.

It was tall with dark, patchy fur, almost as if it had mange. The snout was short, and sharp canines jutted over its bottom lip. At the end of its narrow, spindly arms, were two-inch claws made for tearing flesh.

Werewolf. A strange-looking one, but undoubtedly that was what it was.

It couldn't have been anything else.

I raised my arm to hit it with magic, but the creature pounced first. It ripped through the branches in one giant leap, clearing the trees and hitting me directly in the chest, sending me crashing to the ground.

The monster landed on my chest, sending pain flaring through my arms and legs. Of course I couldn't be lucky enough that the cure Horatio had given me would last longer than one good kick to the pecs, could I?

The creature pinned my shoulders with its long paws. It growled and snapped at me, peeling back its lips to reveal fangs as long as my finger.

Saliva dripped from its canines as it snarled. It pulled back, giving me a one-second warning that it was about to carve my face into tiny steaks.

I hit it with a blast of magic. The creature launched into

the air and smashed against a tree before sinking to the ground.

Werewolves were known to be predictably good on their feet, so I didn't expect it to last long on the grass, and it didn't.

The monster was up, looking at me as if it wanted to attack, but at the last minute it ran off.

Ran off?

Since when did a creature run from a good fight?

Most wanted to destroy you without thinking. But this one hadn't. Why?

And my other question to myself was—was I actually going to allow a werewolf to escape?

No, I wasn't.

I threw magic at the monster to stop it, but it was fast and dodged my attacks. That wasn't going to stop me. I followed it through town and out the other side, where a farm sat. I lost sight of it when the monster slipped into a forest past the farm.

By this time I was out of breath and aching all over. My chest burned and every breath was labored. I couldn't keep going, so I stopped the pursuit.

It was stupid of me to have come this far. The creature could've sliced me in two if it had been given the chance.

As soon as it disappeared into the trees, I slumped onto the grass and waited to see if the werewolf would return. When it seemed like the creature was gone, at least for tonight, I rose and headed back.

Since it had gone past the farm, I was curious if it had come this way earlier.

My question was answered almost immediately. Lying in the middle of a pasture was a sheep. The rest of the flock was huddled in a far corner of the pasture, by a fence. But this one was alone, in the middle, all by itself.

Dead.

THE WITHERING STORM

Even if I hadn't seen the smear of blood on its white coat, I would've known that. But just to be sure...

I jumped over the fence, startling the sheep that were alive. They bleated as I glanced at the house. The lights were still off. No one was awake. Huh. The sheep weren't that loud, but if a predator had entered their midst, which it had, they would've been bleating for help.

But no one in the house was awake. So either the house was empty or the sheep hadn't made a sound.

When I reached the carcass, it was clear that the werewolf had made quick work of it. Bloody footprints tracked from the sheep toward the house.

Horror gripped my heart.

Or maybe it wasn't that the house was empty at all. Perhaps the werewolf had finished off more than one meal tonight.

My footsteps were silent as I approached. The prints led all the way to a window. I peered inside, but it was pitch-black. I couldn't see in.

So I rapped on the glass.

Seconds later a light snapped on. I threw myself to the side of the window so that whoever was in there wouldn't see me.

As I listened, feet hit a wooden floor and padded to the window. The person paused before turning back and getting into their bed.

That was when I ventured a look. What I saw made my blood turn to ice.

A young boy, maybe ten, climbed back into bed and pulled the covers over his head.

He had been who the werewolf wanted to see. Why?

And worse, the creature had left bloody paw prints on the windowsill, as if it had been wanting to devour him, too.

10

"There's a werewolf in the town," I said the next morning at breakfast.

Horatio's fork clattered on top of his plate. "Werewolf? How would you know that?"

"Because I saw it last night."

Red dots bloomed on his cheeks. "You saw it? Where?"

"In town. I went out last night."

Paige shot me a worried look. "Grim, you're not supposed to go out."

"*During the day.* I'm not supposed to go out during the day. No one said anything about night." When no one responded, I kept on. "The creature had killed a sheep, but it was aiming for a little boy in a house."

"And how do you know that?" Horatio asked.

"Because I followed it's bloody footprints to the boy's window."

The TV star stiffened. "You tracked it?"

"Last I checked I was still a monster hunter, same as you. It's out there. We need to find it before it kills someone."

"Yes, yes of course. I'll go out tonight and look for it."

60

THE WITHERING STORM

"I'll go with you."

"Grim, you really need to rest." He forked a pancake from the center of the table and slid it onto his plate before drizzling a river of syrup on top of it. "I can go with my camera crew. Right, boys?"

The camera crew had come in late for breakfast. They gave muffled yeses and nods before taking seats and loading their plates. They were a quiet group that kept mostly to themselves.

I didn't trust them.

"See?" Horatio pinned his focus back on me. "I'll take the crew tonight, and we'll capture this werewolf. At the very least maybe we can run it off."

"Run it off?" Matt frowned. "You've never run a creature off on your show before. You always capture them."

"Well, you can't very well kill monsters on camera, now can you?" he said with a chuckle.

"What do you do with them if you don't kill them?" Paige asked.

"I give them to the council."

"What do *they* do with them?"

"I assume they destroy them."

Her jaw dropped. "All of them?"

"All of them," Drea confirmed over Paige's shoulder as she poured more orange juice into her glass. "All the monsters are euthanized. Isn't that what they've told you, Dad?"

"Yes, it is. But we don't reveal that to our viewers. All they know is that the creatures are captured and treated humanely."

"I'm sure Carrington Dorn is humane," I added, unable to keep the sarcasm from my voice. "So we'll hunt the creature tonight."

"You need to stay here."

61

I narrowed my eyes. "I'm coming with you. You can video this part. Your audience will love it."

"I oversee therapy and treatment," Horatio said through gritted teeth. "And if I say that you need to stay here, then you will. And if you don't like my terms, then you can leave."

Paige shot me a dark look. "He'll stay here. Don't worry. Grim will do what you ask."

I ripped my gaze from Horatio to meet hers. From across the table, Paige was giving me a pleading look. *Please do as he says. He holds the key to making you well.*

I blew a loud gush of air from my lungs. "Fine. I'll stay here while you hunt the creature."

Matt tossed his napkin onto the table with a flourish. "Now that that's settled, can I go with you?"

MATT CLEARLY HAD NO LOYALTY, and Horatio told him that yes, he was welcome to monster hunt with him and his crew as long as he didn't get in the way.

Whereas I was little more than chopped liver.

As soon as breakfast was over, Paige pulled me into the pool room. "Want to play?"

It had been forever since I'd played pool, and a distraction sounded great. So I racked up the balls and let her break.

The balls scattered across the smooth green surface. "Eight ball?" she asked.

"Sounds good to me."

As she played, Paige walked around the table, determining her best chances of not sinking the eight ball into a pocket. "So you went outside."

I sighed and folded my arms. "Is that what this is about? You've brought me in here for a scolding?"

THE WITHERING STORM

She smirked. "I considered bringing you in for a spanking but thought better of it."

"Now that I would've willingly succumbed to."

She laughed before leaning over the table and punching the white ball with her pool cue. A loud *crack* filled the room as it hit its target and the green 6 slid into a corner pocket.

Paige stalked the balls again, and I couldn't rip my gaze from her as she draped her body across the table, her hair falling over her shoulders. The look of concentration on her face was enough to make me break into a sweat. I flexed my fingers to give them something to do other than run them through her silky hair.

"You're staring," she murmured.

"I like the view."

"You won't have this view if you disobey Horatio."

"Who says?"

"He does."

Crack!

Balls spiraled, but none dropped into a pocket. She handed the cue to me, and I deliberately brushed my fingers over hers as I took it.

Her gaze flitted up to meet mine. "I know this is hard for you, doing what he says."

"It's more than hard," I growled, slipping away from her and lining up my shot.

"But you have to listen to him."

"I don't like being blackmailed."

She barked a laugh. "Blackmailed? He's curing you."

"Yeah, at the expense of keeping me a prisoner."

Crack!

The yellow 1 spiraled into a side pocket. I lined up the next shot. *Crack!* Thirteen was gobbled up by a corner hole.

Crack!

AMY BOYLES

Ten spun toward the side but bounced off the rail. I huffed, and Paige took the cue from me. "You're being pigheaded."

I balked. "What did you say?"

"I said exactly what you think that I said. You're being pigheaded. Horatio's told you what you need to do, he's said that he'll find the werewolf and yet you're insisting on doing everything in your power to go against him. You're purposefully sabotaging yourself."

"I'm not sabotaging myself," I growled.

"Oh yeah?"

A crack filled the air as balls spun toward pockets. Paige didn't look to see if she'd snagged a shot before striding to me and stopping with our faces only inches apart.

"I'm not."

She glared up at me. It had been days since I'd run my fingers through her hair, nuzzled my lips to her neck. I missed her. I couldn't have her. This curse was barreling through my body, making it so that I couldn't trust myself around her. But right now all I wanted to do was claim her lips for my own.

"You are too sabotaging yourself."

I'd been staring at her mouth for so long that I'd almost forgotten we were in the middle of a conversation. "And how is that?"

"You're going against what Horatio said."

"I'm trying to potentially save lives." My eyes narrowed. "I'm a monster hunter. I hunt creatures to stop them from harming people, because that's what they do. I'm a living, breathing testament to that."

"I know, but..."

"But you think that this will be different? That the werewolf wasn't pawing at the boy's window because he wanted to eat it?"

Her gaze flashed to the floor. "No, of course not. I'm sure it meant to harm him."

THE WITHERING STORM

"And I would never forgive myself if I could have stopped it from hurting someone and it did."

"But the cure—"

"Paige." I took her shoulders and bent down. She was so small, fragile, like a doll. "He doesn't even have the next part of the cure. He's said so himself. What if this is all I get?"

She peered at me with eyes full of fright. "You don't think he'd do that, do you? Lure you here with promises of curing you but not be able to carry through."

"I don't know. He's a celebrity. Can we really trust him? He only thinks about himself. You saw him at breakfast. He was more concerned about the fact that I'd left the house than he was about a werewolf that might devour the town."

She dragged her teeth over her bottom lip. "You're right. He was."

I dropped my chin to my chest. "Right now he's the only person separating me from this infection. So yeah, I do trust him. I trust him as much as I can. Until I don't."

She reached up and stroked my cheek with her thumb. "I don't know what I'd do if anything happened to you."

I pulled her into my chest and buried my nose in her hair. She smelled like strawberries and...vanilla. That was the other scent that I'd been missing. "I feel the same, and if this infection takes me—"

She pulled her head up. "Don't talk like that."

I swallowed down the lump in my throat. "If it takes me, then know that I loved you. That I've loved you from the first moment we met. That you've given me more joy than I've ever known."

Tears streamed down her eyes. "How did a game of pool turn into this?"

I chuckled and hugged her again. "It's going to be all right. In the end, everything will turn out okay. You've got to have faith, because if you don't, you don't have anything."

She curled her hands into the sides of my shirt. "I've got faith. We'll get through this." She inhaled deeply and pulled back, still gripping me. "But you've got to do as you're told."

"I can't make any promises. Paige"—I shifted my weight from one leg to the other—"there's a creature out there hunting children. It's hunting animals. It could wind up hunting us. I won't be able to sleep at night if something happens to you and I could've stopped it. So I'm promising you right now that I won't stay put."

She bit the inside of her cheek. "What are you going to do since Horatio won't let you hunt with him?"

As I stared into her beautiful eyes, I stroked her hair and tucked it behind her ear. I wasn't in any shape to chase after a creature like a werewolf.

If we met again, the creature would recognize my scent, and this time it would be prepared to fight. It was like the old saying, fool me once, shame on you. Fool me twice, shame on me.

But just the thought of Paige being harmed by the werewolf made me want to hurt something—like the creature. Horatio would probably find a way to up my security so that I couldn't leave—lock me in my room, etc.

But that didn't mean he'd be able to keep me here.

"You're planning to sneak out, aren't you?" she asked. "Even though he's told you not to. Why?"

I shrugged. "Maybe it's because I can't say no to a challenge."

"And maybe it's because you're pigheaded and don't listen."

I smiled. "Probably that."

She rolled her eyes. "Come on. Let's finish this game. I plan to beat you."

I ran my finger over her collarbone. "And I plan to enjoy every minute of it."

11

Turned out that Horatio didn't lock my door, which surprised both me and Paige.

"I want to go with you."

"No." I slipped my belt through the loops and buckled it. "You're staying here."

She folded her arms and glared at me. "I'm keeping your secret, and you're not taking me."

"Trust me, darling"—I brushed my lips over her forehead—"it won't be a secret for very long if that werewolf shows up. I'll be in the thick of it, and you might be hurt."

"But so might you."

I tugged on my jacket. "The difference is that I'm trained in this. You aren't."

"A small inconvenience."

I smirked. "No. End of story."

"Grim, I'm not going to sit by the fire and darn your socks while you're gone."

I clicked my tongue. "Pity. I've got an old pair that need some mending."

"Very funny."

She looked at me expectantly, and I shook my head. "The answer's no, Paige. Stay put. I've got enough on my plate trying to hide myself from Horatio. He might just hand me over to Dorn if he sees me as a liability to him and his crew."

She stared at me for a long minute before sighing. "Fine. But you find me as soon as you come back. I want to know that you're okay and in one piece."

I sat on the edge of the bed and shoved my foot into a boot before lacing it. "I will."

"Promise?"

"Cross my heart."

I put on the other boot and laced it as well. When I rose, Paige eyed me up and down. "You look good. Ready to hunt a werewolf."

I kissed her head. "I'll be back soon."

She grabbed me by the lapels of my jacket, pushed up onto her tiptoes and crashed her lips against mine. When we parted, we were both breathless and my heart was skyrocketing. Another kiss like that and I might just forget what I was supposed to be doing.

"Be careful," she whispered hoarsely.

"I will."

I didn't stay to peer into her eyes or even to give her another hug because if I had, I knew that I wouldn't leave. So I turned my back on her and exited the house, heading into the night.

Horatio, Matt and his crew were nowhere to be seen. I assumed that they'd head straight into town, same as I had, and would encounter the werewolf there.

But I was wrong.

The night was eerily quiet, with just the sound of the

howling wind as I approached town. The lights were off except for the sheep farm, which had more lights on, most likely to scare off the creature that had killed the sheep.

I jumped the fence and padded over to the window that led to the little boy's room and saw that it was no different than the night before. Just the bloody paw prints were on it. There was no sign of forced entry.

Good.

So the boy was safe.

If this was the werewolf's target, then the creature would be back, which meant I needed to stay out of sight and downwind of the beast if I hoped to remain undetected.

So I headed into a tree-lined area and sat down to wait.

I MUST'VE DOZED OFF, because the next time I looked up through the trees and into the sky, the moon was high. The farm was quiet, and there was no sign of Horatio and his crew. Where were they?

Just as I was wondering that, a figure slinked out of the woods across from the farm. I blinked and sat up.

The creature stayed low to the ground, but there was no mistaking that it was the werewolf.

It looked left and right, making sure the coast was clear, before it headed straight for the farm. The sheep paid it no mind, and it ignored them as it headed for the window.

Just as I suspected, the sheep recognized the werewolf's scent. They had to. There was no other explanation for why they would allow the beast to get so close to them.

I watched as the werewolf padded to the window and pressed its paws against the frame. Would the creature be able to get the window up?

Werewolves were ruled more by instinct than anything

else. When a man was in the throes of the beast, he didn't think like a human anymore. He was consumed by the beast within.

But this creature seemed to think clearly. It pushed against the window as if it was trying to get the thing up.

Well, I couldn't have that, now could I?

I pushed my way through the dense foliage until I stood in front of the tree line. The creature's paws scrabbled against the wooden window frame, working in overdrive to break in.

"You have a penchant for wanting things that you shouldn't."

The wolf's head swung in my direction. Its glittering gold eyes landed on me, and the beast slowly lowered itself onto all four paws and snarled.

"I'm not particularly fond of you, either," I told it.

The creature wasn't in the mood for backing down tonight. It looked over its shoulder at the window as if silently saying that it would be back, and then it leaped the fence in one huge bound and raced to me.

I was ready, hitting it with a line of lightning that sent the creature careening to the left. It skidded on its side for twenty feet before digging its massive paws into the ground and coming to a stop.

It rose, shook its head and bared its teeth, saliva dripping from those savage canines.

It leaped at me, racing to attack. I lifted my hand, ready to release a stream of lightning, but nothing came.

I was out? Already? Last night my power had been weak, but I never imagined that I'd be out of magic so quickly.

But there was no time to mourn my loss of magic as the werewolf barreled down. Too bad for me, I didn't have any other weapons. I'd arrived with only my magic.

Stupid me.

I spotted a branch about ten feet away. I dive rolled,

THE WITHERING STORM

grabbed it and would have been able to get up if the werewolf hadn't jumped on me just then.

Wouldn't you just figure?

I pressed the branch into the wolf's mouth. It chomped into the wood, snarling and growling, trying to shake the branch like a dog, but I held fast.

Werewolves can scratch you. They can even draw blood with their nails. Neither of those things will affect you. But if a werewolf bites you and you live, then you take on the curse. There's no way around it.

Since I was already cursed by one creature, I wasn't interested in being infected by another, so with every ounce of strength in me, I got my knees up under the wolf and kicked it off, sending it sprawling back.

The wolf slid across the grass and shook its head as if it had been punched.

It stared at me with glowing yellow eyes that reeked of hatred. The feeling was mutual.

"Stay away from that boy," I told it.

I didn't know how much it understood in its state. My guess was not much.

The werewolf panted and stalked forward. Its three-inch claws dug into the ground as it moved, churning up rocks and earth. I lifted the branch, but it was broken in half, severed by the creature's teeth.

Great.

Now I had no weapon and no magic.

I really hadn't thought this through.

The odds of outrunning the creature were zero to none. It was about a thousand times faster than me. The nearest tree was fifteen yards away. I wouldn't make it before the werewolf had me pinned on my stomach and it was tearing into my back.

One thing was clear—I was rusty. Maybe Horatio had been

right. I shouldn't have come out here by myself. I should've let him lead the charge.

But where was he?

I was staring at the werewolf, and the celebrity monster hunter along with his band of merry crewmen were nowhere to be had.

The werewolf growled and I growled back.

That gave *it* pause and me just enough time to unbuckle my belt, pull it from the loops, and wrap it around my right arm.

Now I was as ready as I would ever be.

The creature leaped, and I lifted my arm, prepared to let its teeth sink into the belt. My body tightened as the werewolf grabbed hold of my arm and threw me onto my back.

Again.

This was getting redundant.

And not in a good way.

Savage anger filled its eyes as saliva dripped from its fangs. The creature pulled its lips back and stared at me. There was little doubt in my mind that it had only one intention—to rip me limb from limb and eat me whole.

I'd pulled back my left arm to punch it in the face when the werewolf dropped me like I was a flaming hot Taki.

Fear flashed in its eyes as it glanced to the trees. It looked at me again before turning and running off toward the same woods that it had come from.

"What the...?"

I rose and unwound the belt, getting a good look at my arm in the moonlight. It was completely unscathed. Not one puncture wound anywhere.

Thank goodness for small blessings.

But what had made the werewolf run?

Grim...

THE WITHERING STORM

The voice slithered inside my head like a snake. My spine went tight, and anger beat inside my body like a drum.

The withering.

I turned around and saw it.

The creature approached slowly, on legs that looked like stilts made of dried cornstalks. Its muscled body looked the same—like withered corn husks wrapped on themselves, twisted and braided into a body that housed no soul, no conscience, no redeeming qualities. Two eyes like dead coals stared out at me, and the withering spoke inside my head again. *Grim...*

Now I knew why the werewolf had scampered off. Part of me wished that it had stayed so that maybe it could've helped me fight off this creature.

But that would've been asking too much, I knew.

However, *the enemy of my enemy was my friend* did have some merit in this case.

Not that I was in the least inclined to associate with monsters, because I was not.

And as if this night couldn't get any stranger, the creature said, *I've come to take you.*

"Take me? You're not taking me anywhere."

You cannot run from your destiny. You cannot run from becoming what you were meant to be.

"You're not my destiny."

The creature tipped back its head and looked like it was laughing, but only a clicking sound came out. *I am your destiny.*

"Why me? Why all this fuss about me?"

I'd been wondering it from the beginning. The witherings appeared in my dreams. They came to me in the flesh—or the husk, as it were. But why invest all this time and energy into haunting me?

The creature cocked its head. *Why any of you?*

Then I understood. It didn't matter who I was. I was infected, and to the withering, that meant it had claim to me, that I was a part of its clan.

I had no interest in being part of anyone's clan but my own.

And I didn't even have a clan.

"If you want me, you'll have to take me," I spat.

The withering only nodded and continued to march forward.

12

So this was where I was at—no weapons, no magic and no armor. It was clear that I was outmatched against a creature that couldn't be destroyed, at least not by any means that were known.

But that didn't mean I didn't have a plan.

Okay, I didn't. This, I was going to wing.

You will surrender yourself to the anger, the bloodlust...

Images filled my head—horrible images of terrible things, and I was doing all of them. The peace, the inner calm that I had experienced after Horatio had given me the first dose of the cure, vanished. What came in its place was an unquenchable thirst to destroy, maim, rip apart anything and everything that I could.

While I was being tortured with horrendous desires, the creature merely stared at me. The thin line that it called a mouth quirked. I swore it twitched in amusement.

That *thing* was enjoying this. It wanted me to be haunted by the evil that lived inside of it. That was its end goal.

It kept approaching as it shot more and more images into my head. I couldn't push them away, and they weren't foreign to me, either. I saw Paige, the woman I loved, crumple to the floor because of me. I saw Matt...

It was unbearable.

And yet the creature kept walking, hand outstretched, ready to do...what? Infect me again?

As it neared, my skin pulsed. My veins popped and quivered, snaking back and forth under my skin. It felt like my blood was boiling from the closeness of the monster.

The infection, which had nearly disappeared, bloomed bright and hot in my chest. Lancing pain sliced down to my navel, and I hunched over, screaming through the torturous agony.

I closed my eyes, acutely aware that any second now, the withering would be close enough to reach out its long, shriveled arm and take me in its grasp.

I didn't have to ask what would happen then. The creature would accelerate the infection. It would turn me into *it* faster than I ever imagined.

I couldn't think. I could barely breathe. My thoughts were as jumbled and jumping as my flesh, which burned from being so close to the creature.

As its footsteps approached, I managed to open one eye and watch as it lifted its arm to grab me.

Being paralyzed from images and searing pain was not the way that I wanted to go out against a withering. I needed a fighting chance, and I didn't have that.

I didn't have anything except a small amount of willpower left.

What would Paige say if she knew I'd been caught by the thing? She'd never forgive me. Even if I was dead, she wouldn't. She'd curse my name until her death because I'd gone against what Horatio said.

As the creature reached out to me with its shriveled corn

THE WITHERING STORM

husk of a hand, I shot my own arm out and thrust my hand into the center of its chest.

This *thing*, this creature, I knew at one time had been a man—or woman, though from the timbre of its voice I guessed it to be male. Which meant that maybe, just maybe, it still had a heart left.

As soon as my hand punctured the fibrous outer layer of skin (if you could call it that), it halted. It didn't scream. It didn't flinch in pain. It simply stopped.

I closed my hand into a fist, surrounding what I thought must have at one time been the creature's heart.

Though to be fair the thing hadn't had a heart in a long, long time.

I yanked my hand out as hard and as quickly as possible.

That was when the creature screamed.

The thoughts of death and destruction that barraged my head came to a screeching stop. The creature stumbled back and fell to its knees. It looked up at me with eyes that for a split second looked far more human than some I've seen on humans.

Then the light inside of them faded, and the creature toppled over, face down in the grass before disintegrating into dust.

I staggered back, taking deep gulps of air that I hadn't even realized I needed. Exhaustion overcame me, but I pushed past it and stared down at the heart.

It was earth colored and spongy, looking suspiciously like Horatio's cure.

"Grim!"

I weakly glanced over my shoulder to see Matt, Horatio and the crew running toward me.

They were coming from town. Where had they been all this time?

Fatigue was washing over me, but I forced myself to stay

upright as Matt reached me. "We saw the whole thing. Are you okay?"

"I'm...fine." I held up the heart. "I got this."

Horatio pushed past the crew, camera lights on, lenses honed in on me. He took the heart and inspected it.

"When I first saw you," he started, "I was angry, as you can imagine. You disobeyed your doctor's orders. No, I know that I'm no doctor, but the restrictions I've given you, I've done for a reason. Yet you ignored them. Fine. Then I saw the withering and of course thought you were dead. But you, Grim, you've outdone us all."

He lifted the heart and smiled, brandishing it for everyone to see. What was he talking about—I've outdone them all?

Horatio grinned. "Congratulations. You've just secured the second dose of the cure."

13

"This is a case of the hair of the dog," Horatio explained when we returned to his house. It was late, after midnight by the time we reached the home.

I could hear waves crashing against the rocks at the bottom of the cliffs when we entered. It was strange the way this house was built here and the village was situated below. Usually places like this were remote. You couldn't grow anything on the rocky soil, but the town seemed to be doing just fine with their flocks of sheep.

The crew had retired to the guesthouse, leaving Horatio, Matt and me to enter the house alone.

Paige was waiting for us. She took one look at me before her gaze swiveled to Horatio. "I see you found each other."

"And it's a good thing we did," the celebrity said, pulling off a pair of leather gloves and dropping them onto a table, "or else Grim might've been in trouble."

"What's that mean?" When he didn't answer, she turned her furious gaze on me. "What's he talking about?"

I rubbed the back of my neck sheepishly. "He just means there was trouble."

"Trouble? What sort of trouble?"

"The kind of trouble where Grim could've gotten himself killed." Matt smirked. "You know what your problem is, Grim? You don't know how to follow directions. You like to walk into dangerous situations that could get you killed."

I growled at him.

Matt lifted his hands in surrender. "Or you could just do as you want and let the rest of us turn a blind eye."

"Something to drink, anyone?" Horatio asked. "Water? Coffee?"

Matt and I took waters, and we sat down in the living room. The curtains were drawn back from the windows, and moonlight bathed the furniture and walls, giving the interior a ghostly glow.

I sat on a couch, and Paige curled up beside me, slid her hand down my arm and entwined her fingers through mine. "Are you sure that you're okay?"

"I'm sure."

"Now, then, as I was saying, this is a case of the hair that bit the dog," Horatio repeated. "To catch you up to speed, Paige, Grim encountered a withering tonight."

She gasped and her hold on my hand tightened. "What happened?"

"Grim killed it," Matt said proudly—and quickly, so that he was the first one to announce the news. I scowled. He grinned at me. "You should've seen it. He reached into the withering's chest and pulled out its heart."

"Its heart?" She turned her body so that she was facing me. "You did that?"

"He did," Horatio said proudly. "And he did it instinctually. Tell me, Grim. What made you think to do such a thing?"

I shook my head. "I don't know. It was the only recourse I had. My power was spent. Magic wouldn't have worked on it

THE WITHERING STORM

anyway. This is the first time I've ever heard of a withering being killed."

"Not the first." Horatio lifted a finger and settled back onto the square leather chair. "But at least the second—that I know of."

"You know of another withering that was killed?" Matt said, frowning. "You didn't tell us that. You're supposed to be helping Grim."

"My friends, if I told you everything that I know, you wouldn't believe half of it. Some things must be left for surprises."

"What sort of surprises?" Paige bit out. "Are you playing games with us, Horatio?"

"No, no. Not games. But if I had told you two days ago that Grim would need to procure a part of the cure himself, because only he could do it, and to do so he would have to kill a withering, would any of you have believed me?"

The three of us exchanged glances. It was Matt who responded. "We would have been skeptical."

Horatio threw back his head and barked a laugh. "Skeptical is the least of what you would have been. None of you would have believed me. You would have most likely walked right out of this house. It's the same thing that the witch did to me when I begged for her help. She gave me the first part of the cure without question, but when I started begging for the next part, she told me it would come to me. And it did. The withering appeared one night because they always do when they want you. Don't they, Grim?"

He waited for me to reply and I nodded. "They seem to know my weakness."

"That's because they're part of you. You haven't just been infected with a standalone virus. The withering virus connects you to all of them. They can sense you. They want you to join them. So of course they'll come for you, hoping to turn you sooner."

"Wait." Matt rubbed his eyes in exhaustion. "How did you know that Grim would be able to defeat it?"

"Because it was the same when the withering came for me." Horatio glanced at the three of us, making sure that he had our attention before continuing. "I'd been with the witch for several days before the creature arrived. I snuck out that night searching for what, I don't know. I just wanted to get out. I was tired of being indoors, tired of staring at the same four walls. I went for a walk, thinking that no harm would come to me, and that was when the withering appeared. Grim, I was the same as you, spent and powerless. The cure might have given me some of my strength back, but I still wasn't at one hundred percent."

He glanced down at the floor and pursed his lips. "I thought for sure that I would die, that I'd become the very creature that I didn't want to be, that I would succumb to the darkness. Yes, Grim, I've told you that I know what you're going through. Don't look so surprised. The darkness is real, and it holds on tight. It's almost impossible to shatter. So when I was faced with the creature, I looked into that darkness and knew what I had to do. I had to take the very life force from it, even if it killed me."

It was exactly how I had felt. I'd been cornered like a dog with my back against a wall. The only power I had left in me was to fight any way that I could.

He continued. "When I plucked that heart from the withering, the same thing happened to it that happened to yours—it turned to dust. I don't know if I had freed a spirit from the throes of evil, but I certainly hoped so. Either way, it was dead. When I returned to the witch, she had wondered when I would ever get the second piece of the cure, but she was glad that I had it."

THE WITHERING STORM

"Wait. Let me get this straight." Matt flared out his arms dramatically. "You were never going to get the cure for Grim. He was always supposed to harvest it himself?"

"As much as I hate to admit it—yes." Horatio pinned his remorseful gaze on me. "Sorry that I had to lie to you. But as I said, telling someone that they'll have to face off against a formidable opponent and win isn't always the way to get what you want."

"But it is one way," I whispered. "If you had told me, I would have believed you."

"Would you? Would you have listened when I said, you, Grim, must get the next piece of your cure because only you can do it? Only you can reach into a withering's chest and pull out its heart? Would you have abided by that rule? You can't even stay inside." He folded his arms and scowled. "Why would I have believed that you'd listen to me then when you couldn't listen to me before?"

"Not going outside and fighting a withering are two different things," I argued through clenched teeth.

"Both require obedience, which you lack."

"I'm not your servant."

"No, but you're a guest in my house and someone I'm trying to heal. Yet every free second you get, you're hunting what you say is a werewolf, one that neither my men nor I saw tonight."

"That's because you didn't go the right way," I shot back.

Horatio's eyes narrowed. He stared at me for a long minute before replying. "We searched the town, and we searched some of the nearby woods."

"It's not my fault you didn't see it. I did."

Paige sucked air. "You did?"

"I did, and if the withering hadn't shown up, the werewolf might've gotten the better of me."

Horatio's tone was full of disgust. "Grim, the werewolf is

none of your concern. I will take care of it. I'll hunt it down. If that creature had sank its teeth into you, you'd be in a worse place than you are now, a part withering, part werewolf hybrid. If that's not enough of a reason to leave the creature be, then I don't know what is. Of course"—he cocked his head in thought—"there's also the chance that the werewolf would simply kill you. After all, one monster can sniff out another."

His flippant tone made me want to wring his neck. "That werewolf is going after a child in town. It continues to stalk the boy's window, and you're making jokes about whether or not the werewolf would let me live? If you take me hunting it with you, we'll find the werewolf, and you'll be able to stop it and keep the town safe. Isn't that what you want?"

"Of course it's what I want. Those people rely on me. Why else would they allow me to live here, with all the cameras and what-not? They rely on my protection."

"Then protect them," I sneered. "And let me help you."

Matt thumbed toward me. "Grim's a great hunter. Even if he is a bit grumpy. Don't count that against him. Inside, he's a big softie." I shot him a look, and Matt quickly added, "Not that I've seen that ooey-gooey interior, but I know it exists."

"It exists," Paige murmured.

I rolled my eyes. None of this was helping.

Horatio suddenly rose. "We'll discuss all of this tomorrow, after we've gotten a good night's sleep. It's late, and I suggest we get some shut-eye. There's a lot to do tomorrow, for you'll be receiving the second dose of the cure."

"I could take it tonight."

He shook his head. "No, no. Tomorrow's better. We'll all be well rested. I'll see you then."

Without another word Horatio left the room. Matt rose and stretched. "I'm tired, too. But I tell you, next time I'm going to stick with you, Grim. Horatio had us going all over the town and woods tonight." He dropped his voice. "To be honest, I don't think he's a very good monster hunter, but don't tell him I said that. Anyway, good night."

"Good night," Paige parroted as he left the room.

The two of us were silent for a long moment before she finally said, "This is getting strange."

"Do you think?" I smirked and settled back onto the couch, shifting to face her. "Which part is strange, the part where I wasn't told that I'd need to get the cure, or the part where he doesn't seem worried about the werewolf?"

She cringed. "Is both a good answer?"

I nodded solemnly. "That heart was larger than the last piece we had. Maybe it's enough to cure me for good."

"Maybe." She paused.

"What is it?"

"It's nothing."

"It's not nothing." I smoothed a strand of hair from her forehead. "Tell me."

She frowned and a little divot formed between her eyes. "It's just that if only a withering or someone who's infected with the withering's curse can pluck the heart from that creature, then how did Horatio get his hands on the first cure you used?"

I scrubbed a hand down my jaw. "I don't know, but I plan to find out."

14

"We're back with your second favorite monster hunter, Grim, who, if you recall from our last episode, has been infected by a withering and has been able to successfully stomach the first dose of the cure." Horatio whipped his head away from the camera to face me. "Tell us, Grim—how do you feel?"

"Fine."

He waited, hoping I'd elaborate, but I didn't. "Well then, if you're feeling fine, are you ready to accept the second dose of the cure, which you so bravely procured for us?" Before he gave me a chance to answer, the television host added, "Drea, I believe we have footage of that, don't we?"

His daughter replied off camera. "We sure do, Dad."

Horatio rubbed his chin. "Audience, what I'm about to show you may be shocking to some. You might faint. This isn't a trick of lighting or any kind of CGI. All of this is real. Last night Grim bravely faced down against a withering...and destroyed it. Now, I won't show you the most gruesome parts. If I did that, we'd be shut down. But I will show you the most dramatic. Roll the footage, Drea."

THE WITHERING STORM

"Yes, sir."

Tonight Drea was taking on the role of producer, a role that, according to Horatio, she often played, though this was the first she had done so with me.

The red light atop the camera dimmed, suggesting that we were no longer live. Horatio sighed and sat back. "They're going to love that footage. From being here with me you've gained a legion of fans just waiting for you to be healthy so that they can greet you out in the world. What do you think about that?"

What did I think? I thought I wanted to be left alone. "That's great."

"And we're back in three," Drea announced.

"Are you ready? We'll be doing it live this time."

I glanced down at the table I was strapped to. My arms were cinched tightly to the examination surface, and the lights were glaring. I had to squint to get a good look at Horatio.

Paige and Matt were in the room. Paige was nibbling the inside of her thumb, probably worried that Horatio's audience wouldn't want me to be given the last part of the cure. Not that this whole thing wasn't rigged or anything like that.

Of course it was. Horatio wasn't going to keep the cure from me.

Horatio beamed at the camera. "Terribly shocking video, isn't it? The part that you didn't see, audience, was when Grim killed the withering. Yes, he killed it, accomplished the one task that's evaded mankind for centuries. But there's a catch— only someone in Grim's condition can destroy a withering. Those creatures are only vulnerable to each other. If I or anyone else had attempted what he had, we wouldn't have been successful. That's how we have this."

He pulled a vial from his pocket and lifted it so that the cameraman could zoom in. "This is Grim's next dose of cure. If you want to see Grim receive it, text 'yes' to the number on

87

your screen. If you'd rather that we slowly watch Grim become a monster"—I fought off the chill that raced down my spine—"then text 'no' to the number flashing on your screen now. We'll be back momentarily for the results."

The results didn't take long to come in at all. Next thing I knew, Drea was showing Horatio a tablet, and they were both nodding.

"Looks good," he said. Then he focused his attention on me. "Are you ready to see what the audience wants?"

"Only if it's good."

He smiled. "You'll be happy." When we returned to being live, Horatio rose, showing the audience the cure. "You've overwhelmingly voted for Grim to continue his treatments. Congratulations, Grim. You will receive the next dose. Are you ready?"

"Yes," I ground out. All this teasing about the cure was giving me a headache. "Let's get this over with."

"After this, audience, there's only one more dose left. You might wonder why one dose isn't enough. Well, that's because this medicine is like antibiotics. Usually you can't just take one dose and be cured of a disease. You must take several for the medicine to get into your blood and successfully kill the infection. That is the case here. Now. Open wide, Grim."

Being fed like a child on live television wasn't my idea of a good time. I would've rather Paige administered the dose to me. But from the corner of my eye I watched her glaring in my direction, silently willing me to be a good Grim and take my medicine.

I opened my mouth, and Horatio dropped what looked like a shriveled piece of fungus onto my tongue. It seemed smaller than it had been when I'd first gotten it.

Horatio must have seen the questioning look in my eyes, because he replied, "It's been dried so it lost some of its volume."

THE WITHERING STORM

Without another word I closed my mouth around the spongy mass, grimacing at the bitter taste as I chewed and swallowed.

Horatio flipped toward the camera. "Let's see how he reacts, audience. Will it be just as savage as last time?"

It was. I wanted to jump out of my skin from the pain slithering beneath the surface of my flesh. I clenched my fists against the wave of agony that rolled through me, but it didn't do anything to ease the fire that wanted to burn a hole into my chest. I grunted against the pain as the cameras rolled, and let breath after staggering breath escape my lungs.

After what felt like an eternity, the waves of agony finally lessened and I was left a limp, sweaty mess.

"Be sure to tune in next time and see how Grim's progressing. Only one more dose, audience, and he will be cured. Until we meet again, may the only monsters you see be those in your sleep."

"And we're clear," Drea announced before dragging a headset down her head onto her shoulders. "Can I get you some water, Grim?"

"Yes," I said weakly.

Paige was beside me quick as a wink. "Are you okay?" She pressed the back of her hand to my forehead. "You're cool, so that's good."

"I'm fine. I just want out of these restraints."

"Can they be loosened?" she asked Horatio.

"By all means." He answered distractedly, too busy glancing at a tablet that Drea had handed him on her way to get my water.

While Paige and Matt loosened my restraints, Horatio was all smiles. "You don't know what your infection has done for my ratings. You've been quite the godsend. I'll admit that in this day and age people don't believe in monsters the way that they used to. I think it's because there's too much technology.

AMY BOYLES

They don't fear anything. They're not worried that the boogeyman will jump out of a closet. But they should be. Monsters are all around."

"You mean like the werewolf in town?" I asked, rubbing the tenderness from my wrists where the straps had held me tight.

Horatio tensed. "Yes, like that. Listen, I told you to leave that to me."

"Fine. I'll leave it to you—on one condition."

"What's that?"

"You let me go outside at night."

The camera crew, including Drea, slipped past us, heading from the room. "See you upstairs?" she said.

Horatio nodded. "Yes, we'll have some supper."

"Outside?" I reminded him.

Horatio glanced at Paige and Matt. "Can the two of you leave us?"

They both looked at me and I nodded. When they were gone, Horatio said coldly, "I know that my methods may not make sense to you, but you have to trust me. You haven't gone through this like I have. Every step that you take is necessary in order to be cured the way that I was. The witch who saw me through to the other side of my infection, the healthy side, she didn't let me know anything. She kept me in the dark, and afterward I understood why. First, I never would've believed what I was supposed to do. If she'd told me that I would meet a withering and grab its heart—"

"Yes, I know. We've already discussed this. You don't think that I would've done it."

His face was red with fury. "Would you even have believed it possible?"

Would I? We were talking about a creature that no one knew how to kill—no one except Horatio Crooks, that was. Yet here I was having just done the impossible.

"You don't give me enough credit."

THE WITHERING STORM

He lifted a brow. "I should say the same to you. Everything I'm doing, it's for a reason—a very specific one, to treat and heal you. You must trust me."

I folded my arms and glared at him. "Fine. I will obey—up to a point. I want to go out at night."

"Not this again about the werewolf."

"I don't understand why you're not worried about it. Shouldn't you be?"

A vein in his temple pulsed. "Of course I am. But you are more important to me than a werewolf."

Wait. What? "It could kill people."

He flicked his hand, dismissing me. "Fine. Yes. I'll take my crew out tonight and every night that I have to, until we catch it. Are you happy?"

Not really. "It will have to do. And you have to let me outside at night. No questions asked."

"Grim," he said my name sadly. "The first dose of the medicine makes things easier. You feel better, and you start to see the light at the end of the tunnel. The second dose is different."

"How so?"

He sank back onto his chair and crossed his legs. Above us, the fluorescent lights hummed, making the only sound that filled the room until Horatio sighed.

"You may see things, hear things that will make you think that you're going crazy. As the withering's hold on you lessens, they will fight harder to keep you. Fighting harder for them means making you miserable. This will be the most challenging part of your journey. Because of that, I can let you go outside at night, but your movements will be restricted. They must be. For your safety and for the safety of others."

Great. So we were back to that again. But if I was going to keep Paige and Matt safe, then I'd do what he said. "Fine."

He nodded, satisfied. "Good. Now. Can I escort you back upstairs?"

"Yes."

I lowered myself onto the floor with shaky legs. That second dose had taken a lot out of me. Horatio knew this and he gently pushed his shoulder into my armpit, offering support.

We made our way slowly to the door, and when we were almost there, a loud *thump* ricocheted through the room.

I spun around, losing my balance and nearly collapsing. Horatio held me tight, grabbing me before I collided with linoleum.

"What was that?"

He lifted a brow. "What was what?"

"That sound. Didn't you hear it?"

He shook his head. "I see the hallucinations are already starting. There was no sound. You imagined it."

I scanned the room, but all was quiet. Yet that sound had been so real, and it had seemed muffled, as if it hadn't occurred in this room but in another.

My gaze sharpened on the far door, the one that could only be opened with the keypad. "What's behind that door?"

"Like I've said, where I try to grow things."

If that was all that it was, then why did Horatio feel the need to keep whatever lay behind it under lock and key?

15

"So how'd you talk Horatio into letting you go outside at night?" Paige asked the next night.

"I wore him down with my shy smile and good looks."

She tossed her head back and laughed. Her dark waves of hair tumbled over her shoulders. "Look at you, using all that charm you've got. I knew you could do it."

I forced a smile to my face. Truth be told, the past day had been more challenging than I'd expected with the hallucinations taking effect. I'd imagine that I was standing beside a wall, and when I'd go to lean against it, I'd find nothing but air.

Do that a few times and you get skeptical real quick when it comes to walls—and other things.

But this was real. Paige and I were outside. It was night-time, and we were sitting on the back deck. Horatio had taken a group out hunting for the werewolf. Since he wouldn't let me track the creature, the next best thing was knowing that he was doing it. Matt had also gone with them, and I knew Matt would tattle if anything strange happened.

Paige grabbed my hand and squeezed it. "How do you feel?"

"Groggy. Like I'm underwater."

A pained look sliced across her face. "I wish all of this was over."

"Me too."

"I know you do. Of course. It's selfish of me to want this for myself. I want it for you, too. I want you to be done with this, and I want you back the way you were—grumpy."

It was my turn to laugh. I motioned to my lap, and she rose from her chair and climbed on top of me, hooking her arms around my neck.

She smelled good. She felt good too, all silky and soft—both her clothing and her skin. My heart tightened just looking at her. Never, not ever had I experienced these feelings with anyone but Paige. I'd had other girlfriends before, yes, and whom I'd loved very much. But Paige made my chest constrict, made it feel like a hand was squeezing the life from my heart—in a good way.

She made me want to live.

And in turn I wanted to.

"It must be killing you that Horatio's hunting the werewolf and not you."

I sighed and slumped back onto the chair. "It wouldn't if I wasn't reminded of it."

"Sorry." She walked her fingers up my chest. "Have you been feeling okay?"

I shrugged. "As well as I can. Horatio hasn't told me any more about what happens next. Am I supposed to kill another withering for the third dose? Is there a third dose?"

"A little transparency would be nice." She pressed her lips to my forehead. "You're doing an amazing job of staying positive."

I tipped my head back and held her gaze. "If it's due to anything, it's due to you."

"I like to think so."

THE WITHERING STORM

I smiled and drank in the sight of her. Paige was what made all of this worth it. Knowing that she was waiting for me was what pushed me. If it wasn't for her, I might've succumbed to the withering's pull long ago.

"They say Virginia's made for lovers, but I didn't also know the cliffs were."

We startled at the sound of Carrington Dorn's voice. He stood on the edge of the patio cloaked mostly in shadow with just enough light slicing across his face for me to make out that it was him. Really him.

At least I thought so. "Is that...?"

"Yes." Paige tensed underneath my fingers. "It's him."

"Go inside."

"No, I'm not—"

"Go inside," I snarled. Anger flashed in my eyes. Frustration and hesitation flashed in hers.

"I don't want to leave you."

"I'll be fine."

"He'll be fine," Dorn parroted.

"He just wants to talk." I gave Paige's arm a squeeze and gently pulled her up. She hesitated but I said, "I'll see you in a minute."

"One minute," she said sternly.

I nodded and she shot Dorn a glaring look before slipping inside the house and out of sight.

"How good of you to lie so well to her," he said, still standing in the shadows like a coward.

"How good of you to show up alone to do what you're going to."

"How do you know that I'm alone?"

"Because how many officers do you know want to go against their childhood hero to arrest someone at his house? Risk Horatio's wrath? Only you'd be stupid enough for that."

He tsked. "You know my men too well, Grim."

"No, I understand human nature better than you do, Dorn. It's pretty simple."

He stilled, and I could almost see anger rolling off him in waves of smoky magic. Almost. He was restraining himself well.

"There's a werewolf in town," I told him. "Perhaps you should help capture it, do something worth your rank."

Dorn lifted his hands and tugged on the black gloves encasing them. "There's already a monster hunter on that one. I assume that's where Horatio is."

"Ah, so you planned for him to be gone when you attacked me."

All this time I hadn't moved. I remained pushed deeply into the Adirondack chair, watching and waiting for Dorn to strike first.

I would have thought him a hallucination if it hadn't been for Paige seeing him, too. Part of me wished he wasn't real. I wasn't in the mood to fight tonight, especially not against him.

Dorn was one of the best magic wielders that I knew. He was also strong as a bull and could throw a punch like a pro boxer.

But if it came down to it, I was scrappier, and scrappy went a long way in hand-to-hand.

"You saw the episode," I murmured.

"I saw it. Those fools think that you can be cured, but I know better. You can't be."

I quirked a brow. "Really? You know better?"

"Of course I do. I've been a monster hunter as long as you, Grim. I've seen what you've seen and then some. Witherings don't let go once they have you. They keep ahold of you. There's a reason why no man can kill them. Why they can only be killed by their own."

"A fact, I'm thinking, you just learned when watching the episode."

THE WITHERING STORM

His shoulders tightened. "My father always said it was important to learn one new fact every day."

The wind was coming in hard from the east. It had just picked up with Dorn's appearance. Even nature didn't like him.

But that also meant that whatever magic he planned to throw my way, he'd have to conjure it hard, because otherwise it would be eaten by the wind.

And since I was farther upwind than him, all I had to do was cast out and my spell would hit him easily.

But I couldn't strike first. Doing that would put me at risk of going to jail.

"Do you even have a warrant for my arrest?"

"I don't need one. You're a menace, a danger to society. I can arrest you on my own authority."

"Is that so? I've never heard that law."

"Grim, when the world sees what you become, they'll thank me for what I'm about to do. Horatio won't be able to hide behind the protection of his celebrity."

"Ah, so that's another way that he's getting away with this —me, I mean. Your superiors have told you to wait and watch."

"I don't care about them."

"And you're willing to go against their commands in order to get what you want."

"You are a danger! If you're allowed to live, you'll wind up destroying people, the same people you've sworn to protect, the same ones that I've sworn to protect. You realize that right now you're being selfish. You're not thinking rationally, Grim. If you were, then you'd turn yourself in and allow us to..."

"To what? Put me down like a dog? Is that what you'd do?"

His head dropped. "It would be for the greater good."

Carrington Dorn would allow a fellow monster hunter, someone whom he had once hunted alongside of—and we didn't like each other then, believe me—but he would allow me to be executed even when I hadn't completely turned.

It was difficult to explain how that made me feel. On the one hand, I understood his position. If you encountered a rabid dog, you put it down because the likelihood that it would spread the disease was high. You were saving others at the expense of one animal that would eventually die anyway.

But at the same time I'd been searching for a cure. I was still clinging to the hope that I could be saved, and Horatio was the one person who had given that to me. It was because of him that I had come this far. I only prayed that there was just one more dose of cure to take and I'd be healed completely.

As much as I understood Dorn's position—and I did—this was my life that we were talking about, and I wasn't going to sit by idly and let him take it from me.

"You'd better move quickly if you want to kill me before Horatio returns. I don't think he'll look too kindly on a trespasser killing a guest of his, one who's also increasing his ratings."

Dorn cursed and stepped forward. "You can come with me without a fight."

"For what? So that I can be destroyed in a cell instead of being killed here? No thanks. I'm not surrendering."

"Have it your way."

Before I was given a chance to blink, the earth erupted underneath me.

Crap. I'd forgotten that he had power over earth. Here I was thinking that he'd throw magic when all he had to do was use the ground to grab me.

I leaped from my chair and tossed a line of lightning at him.

Dorn barely dodged it, jumping out of the way just as my

THE WITHERING STORM

power struck the ground where he'd been standing. The earth exploded up around him.

My attack diverted his attention enough that his attack halted—the ground beneath my feet flattened. Since Dorn had the power of earth, there was no place for me to stand that was safe. I was literally surrounded by a death trap.

The only way for me to defeat him was to incapacitate him.

I shot more magic at him, quickly depleting my limited stores. Dorn rolled and dodged. I couldn't keep this up for very long. Sooner or later I'd have to surrender.

But not until I gave it all I had.

Dorn rose and threw out his hand. The earth rumbled under me, and I jumped away to keep from being swallowed in the pit that opened up at my feet.

Turned out I leaped right into Dorn's expecting hands. Or hand, as it was.

A fist made of earth encircled me, squeezing me in a grip as strong as concrete. My arms were pinned at my sides, making it impossible for me to call on my magic.

He chuckled. "Well, well, well. It looks like the great Grim went down easier than anyone would've expected." For the first time he stepped from the shadows. Sweat sprinkled his face, and his eyes were hard as flint. "Looks like I've done the impossible."

"What? Struck a man when he was down? Admirable of you, Dorn."

He scowled. "You're getting what you deserve, Grim, and you know it. I'm doing the world a favor by taking you out."

"Is that what you call it? Doing the world a favor? If this is doing the world a favor, perhaps you should rethink what a danger to society is, because it's not me."

He smirked. "Nice try, but you can't guilt me into feeling bad for you, not when you're just going to become one of those creatures." He lifted his hands. "Prepare to say goodbye."

Just as he was calling on his power, a rope of lightning shot out of the sky and snaked around both his wrists, cinching them together.

"What?" he cried.

Footsteps approached. "Did you really think I was going to slink inside and let you kill Grim?" Paige said, stepping into the light. "What were you planning to do with me after? Leave me alive?"

Dorn sneered. "It doesn't matter what happens to you. What matters is what I was going to do with him, and he would have been dead. You could have lived."

"How merciful of you," she said sarcastically. "Now, I'm going to show you more mercy than you were going to give him. Leave this house and don't come back. If you do, I can't promise that I won't accidentally use this lightning to steal the life from you."

He glared at her. "If you killed me, you'd bring down the entire wrath of the council."

"And if you kill Grim, you'll bring down my wrath, and I can promise you"—her jaw tensed—"you'll be very, very sorry you did that."

Her voice held so much bite that Dorn's eyes flitted with fear. He quickly schooled his expression. "You'll let me go."

"And you'll leave."

"I will. I promise that this time, I'll go. But next time, Grim, I can't make the same promise."

"Release your hold on him," she commanded.

He did as she said, and the ground crumbled away. When she was satisfied that I was safe, she loosened her hold on Dorn's wrists.

He rubbed them and scowled. "Next time, Grim."

And without another word he vanished into the night, swallowed by the darkness.

As soon as he was gone, she rushed over and wrapped me

THE WITHERING STORM

in her arms. It felt good to be held, and better to be held by her.

She searched me for any sign of injury. "Are you okay?"

"I'm fine now." I ran my thumb over her cheek. "You were supposed to stay inside."

"And let him kill you?"

"I had things under control."

She shook her head. "If you call being encased in a hand made of earth being in control, then wow, you sure had Dorn. I'm surprised he wasn't quaking in his boots."

"Are we fighting?"

"Yes, we're fighting. You're supposed to say thank you, Paige, for saving my life. I really owe you one. Maybe I'll give you my firstborn in thanks. You're definitely not supposed to say that you had things under control when it was crazy obvious that you didn't."

"Okay, maybe I could've used some help."

She gaped at me. "Some help?"

"You sure did get me out of a pickle."

Her jaw dropped. "This just gets worse and worse."

I smirked and pulled her into a hug. "Thank you. You saved my life."

"Finally some appreciation for all the things I do."

My grip on her tightened. "I don't know what I would've done if you hadn't been here."

"You would have died."

"Oh, right. That. Thank you."

She pulled free of the hug and shivered. "Come on. Let's go inside. I don't want to be out here anymore."

"You go in. I want to make sure he's really gone." When she shot me a worried look, I added, "I'll only be a minute. Nothing will happen. Go on."

"You have two minutes. If you're not inside by then, I'm coming out with guns blazing."

I chuckled. "My little spitfire. I wouldn't accept anything less."

Her mouth quirked as if to counter what I'd said, but she didn't argue. "Two minutes."

"I'll be there."

As soon as she was safely inside the house, I walked the perimeter. Everything was clear. Since I had at least one minute left, I headed out past the garage, toward an area with small trees. Very few shrubs of any kind grew this close to the cliff, but a few had managed to survive in the rocky terrain.

I'd just stepped toward them when something glinted. I narrowed my eyes. Had I really seen what I'd thought?

I reached the trees and bent at the knee. Indeed, something had shone from this area. It was a silver bowl that was pushed up alongside one of the trees. Inside the bowl was a meaty bone. It was raw, bloody, obviously fresh.

Horatio didn't have any dogs, so this certainly wasn't for them. That could only mean one other thing—he wasn't trying to feed a dog.

He was feeding a werewolf.

16

"You're feeding it," I growled the next morning.

Horatio, Paige and Matt sat eating breakfast while Drea flipped pancakes atop the stove. Horatio had been reading a newspaper (where did he even find one of those anymore?), but when I showed up, he folded the paper and set it on the table beside him.

"And good morning to you, Grim. To what do I owe your ire this morning, on a day when myself and Matt are exhausted from tracking a werewolf that refuses to be found?"

"It doesn't refuse to be found. You're feeding it," I repeated.

Surprise made his eyes wide. "I'm doing what, exactly?"

"I'm not going to repeat myself for a third time."

Matt spoke around a piece of pancake that he'd just popped into his mouth. "I believe Grim said that you're feeding the werewolf."

"Ah, right. Grim, what are you talking about?"

"I found your little bowl out back. It had a bone in it, and you don't have a dog."

"So that must mean that I'm feeding this werewolf that you insist is stalking around town."

103

I flattened my hands on the table and leaned down. "That is what it means."

"Fine." He pushed his chair back and rose. "I didn't want to do this today, Grim, because I'm awfully tired, but let's go."

"Go where?"

"On a little trip."

Matt jumped up. "I'm coming, too."

Paige started to rise, but I motioned for her to sit. "Stay here. I'll be back soon."

Her gaze dashed from Horatio back to me. "You sure?"

"I'm sure."

Horatio glanced at Drea. "I'll be back in a bit. Please keep my breakfast warm, and have something warm for Grim when he returns."

"Of course," she replied.

"Come, Grim. Let me show you what's going on."

Matt and I followed Horatio to the front door. Horatio plucked an umbrella from a coat tree and handed it to me.

"Take this to protect yourself from the sun."

Matt's brows lifted. I knew what he was thinking—that I'd look ridiculous holding an umbrella when it wasn't raining—but I glared at him, just begging him to say it.

His gaze dropped to the ground.

That was what I thought.

As soon as we were outside and I had the umbrella opened, Horatio said, "Now. Where did you find this bowl?"

"I'll take you to it." I led them from the house to the trees and pointed. "It's right inside there."

He smiled tightly. "I'd like for you to take us there."

"Fine." I stalked forward. "It's right—"

But it wasn't right there. In fact, there was nothing there at all. The grass wasn't even smoothed out from where a bowl would have flattened it.

THE WITHERING STORM

"It should be here. There was a silver dog bowl and inside it was a fresh bone. It hadn't even been cooked."

"Mm hm. Well, it doesn't appear to be here now, does it?"

"There's a simple explanation—someone moved it this morning. Or last night. That's easy enough to explain. Horatio, you're not going to get out of this. You've been feeding that creature."

He simply nodded. "Let's head down to the village."

If there was one thing I didn't like, it was attention, and holding a black umbrella on a sunny day gave me exactly what I hated—and a lot of it.

A few people were driving and yes, they looked at me as I walked.

"They must think you're handsome," Matt joked. "If I were getting as many looks as you, you can be sure that I'd be preening like a peacock."

I grunted.

"You know what your problem is, Grim?"

I sighed. "What problem do I have this time?"

"You can't relax. I realize you've got a lot going on, but sometimes the best medicine is relaxation." I glared at him, and he lifted his hands in surrender. "Okay, never mind. Just ignore me."

"Will do."

Horatio stopped. "This is the home where you believe that you saw the werewolf, correct?"

We stood at the farmhouse. The sheep grazed lazily in the pasture, looking over at us curiously. Even they were probably wondering why I was holding an umbrella on a cloudless day.

"This is it."

"That's what I thought. Come with me."

Horatio knocked on the front door, and a Black man wearing dusty jeans and a plaid shirt answered. He beamed,

105

AMY BOYLES

showing off perfectly straight white teeth. "Hey, Horatio. How're you doing? Long time no see."

Horatio shook the man's hand. "Good to see you, Isaac. This is my friend Grim. He's a monster hunter, same as me, and this is his friend, Matt."

Matt tugged on his lapels proudly. "I'm a monster hunter in training."

Isaac eyed my umbrella quickly, but if he was surprised by it, he masked the emotion expertly. "Great to meet you. Any friend of Horatio's is a friend of ours. Would you like to come in? Have some coffee?"

"No, no. I don't want to burden you. I was just wondering if we could take a look around the farm. We won't disturb anything."

Isaac's eyes narrowed. "Sure, but is everything okay? You haven't gotten any reports of trouble, have you?"

"No, no. Nothing like that."

"Dad, who is it?"

A boy—the same one I'd seen sleeping in the window, ran up. His hair was twisted into small spikes that covered his head, and his brown eyes sparkled with intelligence.

"Raja, you remember Mr. Crooks."

"Yes, sir. How are you?" he asked with perfect manners.

"I'm very well, Raja. My, but how you're growing up. You're going to be as tall as your dad by next year."

Raja, who looked to be around eight or nine, grinned. "That's what my mom keeps saying. She says that I'll be as big as Daddy any day now."

"You just keep eating your vegetables and you'll get there."

"Yes, sir." Raja peered at me. "Why're you holding an umbrella?"

Before I could answer, Matt jumped in to save the day. "Grim here likes to be prepared in case it's going to rain."

THE WITHERING STORM

"But shouldn't you just carry it closed instead of holding it open like that?"

I glared at Matt. "I have a skin condition. I'm allergic to the sun right now."

"Oh," he said as if my reply answered a very important question.

Isaac squeezed Raja's shoulder. "Mr. Crooks is going to look around for a few minutes."

"Can I go, too?"

Isaac started to shake his head, but then he asked Horatio, "Is it okay? Raja wants to be a monster hunter when he grows up."

"Of course he can come. Stay close, Raja. We're on the hunt for tracks."

Raja rubbed his hands with glee. "Let me just put on my boots."

A few seconds later the boy had a pair of muck boots on his feet and a swing in his step.

"Raja, we're looking for tracks," Horatio explained. "Can you let us into the pasture and help us look?"

"Sure thing." The boy skipped ahead and unlocked the gate. He swung it open and bowed. "After you, sirs."

Matt chuckled. "Cute kid. You should have one of those with Paige." When I shot him a hard look, he changed his tune to, "Maybe I'll have one with Shelby."

That gave me pause. "If you can thaw my sister's cold heart, you deserve a medal for bravery."

"She's not so bad. Not once you get to know her. Of course"—he drummed his thumb on his chest—"you have to chainsaw through a layer of ice just to get anywhere close to her heart, and once you're through that layer, there's still another hundred or so to go."

I chuckled. "You're not exaggerating."

"I am not."

107

Once we were through the gate, Horatio spun around, inspecting the space. "Now, Grim, tell me exactly what you saw."

I didn't want to say anything around the boy that would scare him. "Raja?"

He ran up to me and stood at attention. "Yes, sir?"

"Do you have a favorite sheep?"

He swung his head over at the creatures, who stood in one corner of the enclosure staring at us and chewing grass. "I sure do."

"Can you run over and find it, then shout at me when you're standing beside it."

"Absolutely."

Without another word he rushed off and I turned back to Horatio. "I saw a dead sheep there." I pointed to the middle of the pen. "It was lying on its side, gutted. And when I came over here, to the window, there were bloody footprints and scrapes in the wood where its claws had dug in."

"Show me," Horatio requested.

I took him to the window and pointed where I'd seen the marks and the blood. "There."

I stood a distance away. The blood had of course been cleaned up since it had rained in the couple of days since the sheep's slaughter. But the scratches would still be in the wood. You couldn't get those out.

"I don't see anything," Horatio murmured. "Matt, can you take a look?"

Obviously he wasn't looking hard enough. "They're there."

Matt eyed the window and frowned. "Take a look, Grim."

Both men stepped back as I took their spots. My gaze washed over the wood, looking for scratch marks, the ones that I had seen, but they were gone.

I ran my finger over the surface. "They were here. The

marks. The werewolf had pressed its paws to the window frame and looked in on the boy."

"I found him," Raja yelled. "Come and meet Benny!"

"We'll be right there," Horatio called.

Matt gave me a pitying glance. "I'll go meet Benny."

As soon as he was gone, Horatio sighed and shook his head. "I'm sorry to tell you this, and I didn't want to have to. I hoped that maybe you'd leave this werewolf thing behind. Don't you have enough to worry about with the withering?"

"What do you mean, leave this whole werewolf thing behind?"

"What I mean is—we've been out for two nights looking for the creature, but we haven't seen any trace of it. I've catered to you, but this is where it must stop."

"What are you talking about?"

Horatio slipped his hands in his pockets. "Sometimes, the witch told me, the delusions start earlier than the second dose. It's rare, she had said. Since you, my friend, are the first person I've ever cured of a withering infection, I didn't know what to expect, but I'm quickly learning."

All his rambling was giving me a headache. "You're not saying what I think you're saying—that there is no werewolf."

"Of course I am. You're the only person who's seen it. The only one. There is no werewolf. There's no trace of it here, and when we spoke to Isaac just now, did he mention anything about a dead sheep? No, he didn't."

"That doesn't mean—"

"Yes it does!" His face turned crimson. "If his sheep had been gutted, like you say, by a werewolf, then Isaac would have put two and two together—that our visit is because of that killing. But he didn't say one word, and that's because it didn't happen. Grim"—he eyed me with more pity than Matt had—"there is no werewolf. All of this—seeing the creature, the dead sheep, the blood tracks and claw marks—all of it is part of the delusion of the cure. None of it's real. Not one thing. I know this may be hard to accept because it all seems so very, very tangible. But it isn't. None of it is. Can you accept that?"

None of it had happened. It was a blow that struck me hard. How could it have been my imagination? It had all felt so real—fighting with the werewolf, seeing the blood. I'd even smelled it. But Horatio had been hunting the monster for two nights and he hadn't seen hide nor hair of it. It had only been me.

I ran my fingers over the window frame, making sure that I hadn't missed a claw mark or a scratch—something that would justify what I believed was the truth.

But there was nothing there. Nothing.

Horatio was right. I'd conjured the delusion from my own mind, created it out of thin air.

Suddenly everything seemed wrong. My chest was tight; I couldn't breathe. The world was spinning.

"Grim, are you okay? Grim?"

"Yes, I'm..."

But the world was so blurry and my head was so light that I couldn't focus. Everything was dimming. My vision became fuzzy until everything went black.

17

hen I woke up, I saw airplanes suspended from the ceiling. What the...?

The sound of padding feet dragged my attention from the airplanes, and I glanced over to see Raja cocking his head as he tiptoed to me.

"You're awake. I was trying to be quiet."

I quirked a brow. "Have you been staring at me for a long time?"

"No." He tilted his head, studying me as if I were a rare species of human. "Maybe. This is the first time a monster hunter's ever slept in my bed."

I glanced down at the single mattress draped in a superhero blanket. "It's very comfortable."

"Thank you. I make it every day," he told me proudly.

"As much as I like being here, why *am* I here?"

"Oh, you fainted."

Fainted. How typical. A man learns that he's been hallucinating a monster, and he can't handle the truth so he faints. Sounds like a moment from a psychological thriller movie.

"Here. My mother sent some food in. Are you hungry?"

"What've you got?"

Raja lifted a cloth covering a bowl. "Looks like pinto beans and corn bread."

"Any pepper sauce to go with it?"

He grinned. "Right next to it."

"I'll take it."

He brought the tray, and I placed it atop my lap. The beans smelled delicious, like my mother used to make, and the cornbread was a perfect golden brown. "I'll have to thank your mother." I sprinkled some pepper sauce on the beans, crumbled the cornbread on top and took a spoonful. This meal brought back good memories from my childhood, the kind when my parents were still alive. After a few bites in I said, "Why am I here? And where is Horatio?"

The boy climbed up on a stool and watched me closely as if to make sure that I was eating his favorite meal correctly. "He and Matt went back to his house. They left you here because of your condition."

I raised my brow. "My condition?"

"Why you had the umbrella."

"Oh, *that* condition." I took another bite, and it was just as good as the first. "They didn't try to magic me away."

"Mr. Crooks said it was best to leave you here. He'll be back for you tonight—that's if you don't go home yourself."

Paige was probably worried sick, but I didn't have a phone on me or any way to contact her. Matt was probably doing what he could to calm her.

I needed to be gone before darkness fell. There was no telling if the witherings would be coming for me tonight, and I didn't want to lead them straight to this house.

"Did you find what you were looking for?" the boy asked.

"What do you mean?"

"When you were looking at my window. Did you find what you needed?"

THE WITHERING STORM

"Not really."

"Oh." He sounded as disappointed as I felt. "Well, if there's anything that I can help you with, just let me know." He thumbed his chest proudly. "There's nothing that goes on here that I don't know about."

"Is that so?"

"Yep. I let the sheep out every morning to pasture, and I help Daddy bring them in each night. We got to keep them close because of predators."

"Yeah, you would have to do that."

He nibbled his bottom lip as he watched me eat. "What's it like being a monster hunter?"

"Dangerous. Scary."

"So it's a lot like herding sheep."

"I guess that's right. You have to protect them just like I have to protect people from harm. Creatures can harm folks."

"I know. I've seen it."

My brow wrinkled in worry. "You've seen it?"

"Sure, on TV. Everybody watches Mr. Crooks. Thank goodness he lives nearby. No monsters would dare come close to where he lives unless they want to be sliced and diced!"

I chuckled. He was too cute. "You're right. No monster does."

"Then why do they hurt us?"

I took another spoonful of beans and cornbread, trying to come up with an answer that would help him understand the crazy world that we lived in. "Well, everything wants to live and survive, right? Tigers and lions want to live like we do."

"I guess."

"Have you watched a nature show where lions attack?"

"Oh yeah, I've seen that." His eyes lit up with excitement. "They chase down an animal, a whole bunch of lady lions. They catch it and eat it."

"Right. Are they doing that for fun?"

"No, they're doing it because they have to eat."

"Or else what happens?"

"They die."

"Exactly. So they kill and eat to survive. Monsters—what we think of as monsters—they're the same. The only problem is that they kill and eat *us*—little boys and big men included. So we monster hunters have to protect people. I want to stop creatures from hunting and killing my friends. Most monsters are only doing what their instincts tell them to. Do you know what the word 'instinct' means?"

"It means what you do because you have to."

"Right. Most monsters are only following their instincts, and those instincts often lead them to people to kill them. So I have to stop that."

He hung his head. "That's sad. A monster's only trying to survive."

"Would you be sad if a lion killed your best friend, or would you want the lion captured?"

His eyes flared with fear. "I'd want that lion captured."

"It's the same with monsters. We can't show them mercy only because they were just doing what their instincts told them to, because those instincts can cause innocent people to die. People are more important than monsters. Our lives matter more because we talk to one another, we mean something to each other. Monsters don't care for one another like we do. They aren't capable of it. They're creatures that are driven—er, they do what they do because they only think about being hungry and where to find shelter. They don't have the brains to make homes. Monsters are feral. That means they're wild animals."

"I know what it means."

Smart kid. "So it's not that anyone wants to hurt monsters. I don't want to hunt them for the sake of hunting. I hunt them to keep everyone else safe. That's what's important."

THE WITHERING STORM

Raja stroked his chin. "I never thought of monsters like that. I mean, I knew they were bad, at least most of them. But I never really thought about it in terms of keeping others safe because monsters can't control their instincts."

"We humans try to do better, but sometimes even we're not that great at control."

He cocked one eye. "You know what, Grim? You're pretty smart."

I smiled slightly. "You're pretty smart, too."

At least I had thought so until Horatio told me that I'd imagined the werewolf. How could I have made up something like that? How could I have imagined it? It had seemed so real —our fighting, the way it sounded. All of it had been real. But it was only the symptom of the cure fighting the infection. It made me wonder—what else had I imagined? What else wasn't real?

I took a bite of food, not wanting to think about it.

"Do you have any stories?" Raja asked.

He'd been so quiet I'd almost forgotten that he was still in the room. "What kind of stories?"

"The kind where you defeat nasty old monsters?"

"I suppose that I have one or two of those."

His face brightened. "Can I hear one?"

I smirked. "What would your mother say about me telling you monster stories?"

"She'd be okay with it—as long as they're not too scary."

"Hm. How about I tell you one that isn't too scary, then, but is completely real."

His grip on the stool tightened. "That would be *sick*."

So I told him a story about a time when I was on my own, hunting a monster that was damming up the water supply to a farmer's herd of cows. "In the end, the monster hadn't actually hurt anyone or any of the cows, so I relocated it to a different spot, a place where it could dam up the water and live happily."

Raja frowned. "You mean that you didn't kill the monster?"

"In that case, no, I didn't."

"Doesn't that go against everything that you just told me about them? That they're evil, terrible creatures who need to be destroyed?"

"It sort of does—but that water monster wasn't harming anyone, and it wasn't going to. It ate fish most of the time."

He nodded but still frowned. "I guess that makes sense. It's kind of like me."

I took the last spoonful of beans and placed the tray to the side of the bed. "What do you mean, it's kind of like you?"

He smoothed a hand over his hair. "Oh, nothing. I don't mean nothing by that."

"Now you've got me curious. You're saying that the water monster is like you. How so?"

"No, not the water monster is like me—the farmer is like me. He had a monster that showed up, but it didn't harm him."

A tingle started on the back of my neck and worked its way to the top of my head. "What do you mean, that's like you?"

"Well, sometimes at night a monster visits."

If I'd been holding the spoon, I would've dropped it. "What does it look like?"

His gaze darted to the floor. "I'm not supposed to talk about it. Daddy says so."

"What if I ask you questions about it—yes and no questions, that way you're not really talking about it?"

This was going against a code I had—never get kids to betray or go against their parents. It wasn't right unless a child's safety was a concern, and in this case a child's safety was very much a concern—*my* concern.

He nodded, silently giving permission for me to go ahead. "Do you see a monster at night?"

THE WITHERING STORM

He slowly rocked his head up and down.

I exhaled a shallow breath. "Is the monster covered in dark fur?"

"Yes."

"Is it a werewolf?"

"Yes."

My heart was thundering against my rib cage. There *was* a werewolf.

"Do your parents know?"

"Yes."

"Do they believe you?"

"No."

My mind spun. Why wouldn't they believe him? They knew monsters existed, so why wouldn't they think their son was telling the truth? As quickly as I thought it, the answer came to me.

"Has Horatio Crooks promised that no monsters will come to this town because of who he is? Because he keeps you protected?"

"Yes."

My heart fell.

"Is one of your sheep missing?"

He nodded.

"This isn't yes or no, but can you tell me what your father thinks happened to it?"

"It got out of the pen. There's one corner where the fence is broken. The sheep must've gotten out there."

"Has anyone found it?"

He shook his head.

"Raja, this is very important—maybe the most important question that I'm going to ask you, so think very carefully before answering."

"Okay."

"Did you see this werewolf at your window the other

night?"

He didn't hesitate. "Yes."

So I was right. I'd been right all along. It was Horatio who was wrong. Had I been right about the feeding bowl, too?

Yes, of course I had. Horatio was lying about the werewolf —but why?

Was it because of his ego—that a creature had come into his town and he couldn't find it? Was the feeding bowl a trap to ensnare the creature? Or was something more sinister going on—was Horatio feeding the creature for some other reason?

"Raja, have you told anyone else about this creature?"

"No." He opened his mouth to speak, stopped and then started again. "There's something else." Raja dragged his gaze from the floor until our eyes met.

"What is it?"

"The werewolf, when it comes to my window, it scratches at it."

"Yes."

"I think"—his lower lip wobbled—"I think that one night it's going to get in, and when it does, it'll eat me."

18

No way would I allow Raja to be eaten. Before I left his house, I made sure to add a layer of sealing magic to his window to keep the werewolf at bay.

I added a little extra, too, a burning spell. So if the werewolf touched the windowpane, its paws would burn. The marks would last until after the creature transformed back into a human. There would be no way to hide those marks except with gloves.

After that, I said goodbye to Raja, thanked his parents for letting me rest and then I grabbed the umbrella and headed back up to Horatio's house.

I met Paige halfway on the path. Her long cardigan was unbelted, and the tails flapped behind her, picked up on the wind that rolled in from the ocean.

The relief on her face when she saw me made my heart tighten. She threw her arms around me and pressed her face into my chest.

"You're safe," came her muffled words.

"I'm safe. You didn't have to come for me."

She pulled back and tipped her head up, scowling at me.

"Of course I had to come for you. I had to make sure that you were okay. Matt and Horatio just left you in town."

"It was for the best. They didn't want to teleport me. There's no telling what the infection could've done if I'd been transported. Would the magic inside of me make the portal unstable?"

"Well, they could've thrown you in a wagon or a car."

"It was fine," I assured her.

"Not to me, it wasn't." Her gaze searched me. "Are you sure that you're okay? Because when they told me that you'd passed out, I—" Tears sprang from her eyes, and she quickly knuckled them away.

"Shh. I'm okay, Paige. There's nothing to worry about."

"Of course there's something to worry about. There are no guarantees that...everything will be..." She flapped her hand. "You know..."

This wasn't how Paige had been talking a few days or even hours ago. "What happened? What's got you so coiled up?"

"It's nothing."

She looked away, and I hooked a finger under her chin and gently lifted her face until she was forced to meet my gaze. "Tell me."

She sighed and wrapped her arms around my waist. Her flowery scent trickled up my nose, and I buried it in her hair. I couldn't get enough of Paige, and I didn't want to. I wanted all of her, and I wanted her close every minute of every day.

"Horatio acted like it was no big deal that you'd passed out. Matt wanted to bring you back. He'd asked Horatio if there was any way that they could transport you, but Horatio insisted that you'd be fine. You'd stay with those people until you woke up, and that you'd be back sooner rather than later. I guess he was right, but Grim"—her expression pinched in pain —"he didn't seem to care. He wasn't worried about you at all."

"He doesn't have to be."

THE WITHERING STORM

She pulled from me and nodded absently. "I know he doesn't have to be concerned, but why wouldn't he be? He's using you to make money, to help his brand. So why wouldn't he care?"

"Maybe because I'm looking too closely at something he doesn't want me to."

She pulled back and studied me. "What are you talking about?"

"Come on. Let's walk."

We headed away from the house to get some privacy. I told her everything that I'd learned from Horatio, that there wasn't a werewolf, that it had all been my imagination.

"Matt told me that. He was afraid as much, since they hadn't seen any tracks," she said quietly.

"Ah, but this is where it gets interesting." Then I told her what Raja had confessed. "There is a wolf, and it's targeting Raja as its prey—probably because he's young and would make an easy meal, not put up too much of a fight."

Paige's eyes became big as plates. "But Horatio said—"

"I know what he said, but he's lying."

She inhaled a staggering breath. "Why would he lie?"

"I don't know. But he's gaslighting me, wanting me to believe that I'm imagining everything," I growled. "There's a werewolf lurking around, one that's targeting a child, and Horatio's not doing anything about it."

"But why? I don't understand."

"I don't, either," I replied, gritting my teeth. "But I plan to find out."

"How?"

"If I have to sneak out every night until I capture that werewolf, I will."

"I don't know. That's not safe. What about the withering? You killed the one, but what if more appear next time? What if

AMY BOYLES

they know you killed one of them, and so they bring rein-forcements?"

"It's a risk I have to take. For a *child*, Paige. I have to do it for him. No one else believes him, not even his parents."

She dropped her face into her hands. "Horatio's got them all convinced it's nothing, huh?"

"He's very powerful. Celebrity means something around here."

"It means something everywhere," she grumbled.

"There's something else."

"What?"

"I may have been hallucinating, but when I was downstairs, it sounded like something was moving in the room behind the steel door."

She stared at me in surprise. "What are you saying?"

"Horatio told us that room was for growing the fungus. If it's for that, why would any sounds come from there?"

"They wouldn't." She shivered and tugged her cardigan closed. "Maybe you should find out what the last part of the cure is, if it's the same as the rest, and then we can go."

"This morning I would've said yes to that, but now there's a boy who might be in danger, and an unsuspecting town."

Paige glanced off into the distance before looking at me with hard resolve in her eyes, resolve that suggested she'd already made up her mind. "They might not be in danger. No one's been hurt by the werewolf."

"*Yet.*"

"But don't you think that's saying something?"

She was looking at me with those doe eyes. She didn't want to get involved. I understood the feeling because I didn't want to get involved. I'd never wanted to be involved. All I'd wanted was to be a monster hunter in a small town. I hadn't gone looking for this infection.

THE WITHERING STORM

"If you want to leave," I told her, "you can. I won't stop you, and I won't hold it against you."

"I don't want to leave."

"But you don't want to stay."

She shut her eyes and pinched the bridge of her nose. It was all so difficult. It was more than we'd signed up for.

"I won't leave you," she explained.

"You don't have to stay."

"Dang it, Grim, would you just let me say what I want to say?"

I lifted my one free hand, the one not holding the umbrella, in surrender. "Go on."

"If we knew for sure that another withering heart was the key to saving you, I'd say let's leave. But Horatio hasn't told us. Why?"

"To lord over us and make it so that we have to rely on him."

"Right. We have to rely on him; that's what he wants. Maybe we can convince him to tell us for sure what the last dose is and we can leave."

"Paige, I'm not leaving without that werewolf being taken care of—caged or otherwise. Horatio's covering up its existence. There's no way that Raja's parents would allow him to stay in his room with that monster hunting him, and let me be clear—the boy is being hunted."

She sighed. "So we're staying, and you're on a mystery."

I closed my eyes. Just the sound of her exhaustion was enough to make me exhausted, too. "I know this isn't what we wanted. I know it isn't how we expected everything to happen, but this is the hand that we've been dealt."

She raked her fingers down her face. "So what do we do first?"

I didn't want to drag her into this, but I had to keep her

and Matt safe. The way to do that was to make sure that they knew as much as I did.

And to be fair, I didn't know much.

Since it hadn't been long since my second dose of the cure, I had time to find out exactly what was needed for the third dose. I would need that time to stop the werewolf before it could hurt Raja, and to find out what Horatio was hiding.

This whole thing could go south, and quickly. So the first piece of information I needed was to know exactly what the last cure was. If Horatio would give me that information, then nothing else mattered. I could capture the werewolf and not be concerned with how the celebrity monster hunter reacted, because I wouldn't need him anymore.

But the fact was, I did need him—more than I liked to think about.

"You need to know about that last cure, don't you?" Paige asked as if she could read my mind.

"Yeah."

She patted my shoulder. "Leave it to me."

"Leave it to you?"

"Sure. Unless you'd like to guess what it is. Maybe it's another heart. Maybe there isn't a third dose. Maybe Horatio's lying. Did you consider that? You are good for ratings."

I grunted out, "I've thought about it."

"But we won't get the answer from him."

"We won't? If that's the case, then what's your plan?"

She clicked her tongue and with a twinkle in her eyes, said, "Stay close and you'll find out."

With that, Paige winked at me and turned around, heading back toward the house. My instincts screamed at me to leave then, to take her and Matt and go, never return. But she was right—until I knew for sure how to survive this infection, I needed Horatio.

But if he wasn't going to tell me what the third and final dose of the cure was, then who would?

As Paige marched back up the hill toward the house, I realized exactly who she planned to ask—or at least attempt to ask.

Drea.

Horatio's daughter knew the answer. Horatio trusted her implicitly. He would've confided in her what I needed to be fully healed.

But one question remained—would Drea tell us? Or would she keep that knowledge to herself?

My grip on the umbrella tightened as I pointed myself in the direction of the house and set off to hopefully get the answers that I needed.

Only time would tell if I was so lucky.

19

"You're back," Horatio said, arms wide, when I entered the house. "Sorry for leaving you there; you can imagine that I worried you were too unstable to move given your condition and all."

"Yes, I imagine."

He motioned me to a chair. "Did they take care of you? Of course they did. Isaac is a good man," he added as he pulled a stethoscope from thin air and proceeded to press it against my back in various spots. I breathed hard just for him. "I knew you'd be in good hands. But I'm sure you were wondering why I left."

"It did cross my mind."

"Well, you see…" And there he trailed off as if trying to pluck a lie from the air. "I had to get back. Drea and I have show duties. Matt asked to stay, but I told him that there was no telling how long you'd be out. When I underwent my own healing, when the hallucinations began, there were times when I'd faint. I always came to within a few hours."

"But with the witch with you."

He was standing in front of me, and his gaze fell to the

THE WITHERING STORM

floor in what seemed to be guilt. "Yes, she was there, I admit. But I knew you'd be fine, and if you weren't back by dark, I was going to get you myself."

"That's true," Matt said, entering the room. "I made him promise that." Matt leaned against the wall and folded his arms, a pained expression on his face. "How're you feeling?"

"Better." Horatio tried to press the stethoscope to my chest, but I brushed him aside and rose. "I feel much better, and I wanted to talk to you about the final dose."

The celebrity hooked the instrument over his neck. "Yes? What did you want to talk about?"

"What is it?"

Horatio's gaze flicked to Matt, who scowled. He wanted to be in here for this. He must've been feeling as raw as I was. I sighed and nodded to Matt.

"I'll be outside," he told me.

Horatio pulled the door to the den closed and sat on a chair in front of me. "Paige came in a few minutes ago and said that you were on your way up. I told her that I'd take care of you. She didn't look happy about it, but she said she had other things that needed her attention."

Like tracking down Drea. So that's where she'd gone to. "Why're you telling me this?"

"Because I could tell by the look on her face, as well as yours, that there were things you both wanted to discuss, and I'm not surprised that this is it."

It was one among so many things. "You are keeping information from me."

He tutted. "There are reasons. Like I said before, if I'd told you how to get more of the cure, would you have believed me? Would you have done what you did?"

"I might have died," I seethed.

"I think not."

The flippancy in his voice made my hackles rise. "This isn't a game, Horatio. This is my life, and more than that, you're playing with other people's lives, too. What if I hurt someone?"

"Has that urge occurred?" he asked in a voice that suggested he knew the answer.

"No."

"I know what I'm doing."

Do you?

"All will be revealed tomorrow night. We'll have the final show, and the final dose of the cure will be shown to you. Everything that we're building toward will save you. You'll understand why I've done everything the way that I have."

Would I? "Why not just tell me now? Why make me wait at all?"

He sighed and shook his head as if he were explaining things to a child. "Part of this is theater. I'm not going to lie. Seeing your honest reactions as things happen makes it all the more realistic for you and the audience."

"Heaven forbid we forget about the audience."

His face reddened in anger. "You agreed to it, I'll remind you. You must have faith, faith that I'm doing what is right, and that everything is going according to plan—because it is. It's all working the way that it should. Now, we just have to make sure you don't keep having any more of those pesky hallucinations, and everything will be fine." He paused, waiting for me to react. When I didn't, he continued. "How are you feeling, by the way? I know it was difficult discovering that there wasn't a werewolf, but now you know. How're you coping?"

This was where I had to put on my show. So I inhaled deeply and nodded. "It's hard to accept, but everything you showed me seems like yes, I was hallucinating. There isn't a werewolf. I know that now."

"Good," he said, looking pleased, either with me or himself.

THE WITHERING STORM

Hard to know which. "Well then, I've got some things to do a few towns over. I'm heading out, but I should return by dinner. Drea will be here if you need anything."

"What about the camera crew?"

"Oh, they're going with me. We're doing a little research for a site. They'll be staying on, too. They won't be here for tomorrow's filming. Drea will be in charge. I can tell by the look on your face that you're not convinced one person will be enough to run things. Drea's had to film all by herself when we've been in a pickle before. It's hard, but she's great at getting everything set up. Anyway, if I'm not back by dinner, please don't hesitate to start without me. Sometimes scouting takes longer than I plan." He brushed an invisible speck of dust from his trousers. "Is there anything that I can do for you in the meantime?"

He was leaving us alone with Drea? If Paige hadn't already cornered her, I was going to.

I shook my head. "No. There's nothing that you can do for me. Absolutely nothing."

20

_H_oratio was true to his word and didn't make it back in time for dinner. Drea made a light meal of salmon topped with pesto and artichokes along with pasta and a salad.

"This looks delicious," Matt admired.

"I helped," Paige said, entering with a pitcher of iced tea. She sidled up to me and whispered, "Buttering her up."

I gave her a wink. "Anything I can help with?"

"No, we've got it under control." Drea set a tray of steaming rolls on the table. "You know, 'cause we don't have enough carbs with the pasta."

Matt placed a hand over his flat stomach. "I like carbs. Grim likes them too. Don't you, Grim?"

"My favorite." I slid out a chair for Paige. She thanked me before sinking onto it. "Drea, it looks like you outdid yourself."

She smiled feebly and sat at the foot of the table. Horatio's chair was open as if even though he was gone, everyone was afraid to sit there.

THE WITHERING STORM

"My dad doesn't like salmon," she confessed. "So I took the opportunity to make it."

"What will he eat when he comes home?" Matt asked.

"Oh, he'll eat out." She slipped a spatula under the large salmon fillet and plated a slice of it. She handed the plate to Paige, who passed it to me. "He knows that when he's not here, I tend to eat things that he doesn't like."

She giggled as if this was some sort of inside joke. Paige shot me a look that questioned Drea's sanity. I hitched my shoulder in a shrug.

When everyone was served, Drea adjusted her glasses and smiled. "Let's eat."

She picked at her food, taking small bites and focusing solely on the meal. Under the table, Paige nudged me with her foot.

I frowned. "Drea, so um, how long have you been working with your dad?"

She tilted her head in thought. "I guess since I was little. He's always included me on his trips and stuff. It was only a matter of time before I started producing and directing his shows. I don't direct them all, just some of them."

"Oh? Is there a reason for that?" Paige asked brightly.

She shrugged. "Sometimes my schedule doesn't allow for it. Like today, I could've gone with him, but..."

"But what?"

She glanced around nervously. "Well, for one, I have to stay with you three so that you're not abandoned." She giggled again as if that was hilarious. "And for other reasons, I have work to do. Work to prepare for the show tomorrow. It's gonna be a big one."

"That it is," I said.

Her eyes sparkled. "Are you ready for it?"

Here was my in. "In some ways, but you know, what did

you father tell you about when he was sick with the withering infection?"

Her gaze dropped back to her plate. "Not much."

Lying. She was lying. She knew a lot more than she was saying.

"But I'm sure he told you some things," Paige pushed. "You know, about what he went through."

She pushed her food around on her plate. "He did tell me some things."

"Like what?"

She lifted her gaze and met Paige's. "Well, he told me about the witch and about the doses of medicine he had to take. And of course he told me about having to take the second dose from the withering."

And there she stopped. I waited, my heart drumming, for her to continue, but she did not.

"Seems like a lot of mystery surrounding it." Paige picked up the tea pitcher and poured more into Drea's glass. "I know that if I was infected with a disease like that, I would want to know what's coming."

Drea's head snapped up. "Would you?" The look in her eyes suggested that she was inches away from leaping on Paige and attacking.

Paige withered. "Yes, I would want to know."

"Wouldn't you, Drea?" I said soothingly. The feral look in her eyes dimmed, and I released a breath. What was that about? "If you were infected with a disease like I am and it was something that could be fixed at a hospital, a doctor would tell me exactly what the treatment was going to be. He would tell me what I would be taking, the side effects of it—all of that. There wouldn't be anything left for me to discover on my own."

"Perhaps." She slumped back into the chair and poked her fork at the salmon. "But maybe the doctor would know that

THE WITHERING STORM

you'd undergo great suffering, so he wouldn't tell you—couldn't, because of that. Because the doctor knew that you'd run scared if you knew anything about what was going to happen to you. Even if you'd lived your entire life happy and secluded, when it came to your medicine, you had to take it. You knew that it was what was best for you, so you go along with it, and you continue to go along with it, always doing what you're told because you're good and that's what good people do."

Fire flared in her eyes, her head was tipped down, and she looked an inch away from leaping across the table and jumping out the window.

What was happening?

"What is it that you really want to know, Grim?"

I debated for half a second lying, but she was on to us, so there was no point. "What's the third dose? Is it another heart?"

She shook her head. "I can't tell you."

"Can't or won't?" Matt asked.

She considered the question. "Both."

Matt gripped his fork until his knuckles whitened. "Why not? This is a man's life we're talking about."

"Because sometimes the best gifts are surprises. It's when you don't know what's inside the box that you're the most delighted when you open it. If I told you what was going to happen, then that wouldn't just spoil the surprise, it would ruin everything. In this with the withering, you can't know, Grim. It's part of it—not because I'm trying to be devious, but because it's the only way to go through the experience and come out the other side healed."

"So it's like Neo and the Matrix. You can't know what the pill's going to reveal before you swallow it," Matt mused.

"I have no idea what you're talking about," she said.

"Never mind." Matt smirked. "I thought you were more

like a Miss Teschmacher from *Superman* than that—that you'd help Grim."

Drea looked at each of us in turn before answering. It was unnerving the way her gaze skated over our faces before it finally landed back on her plate. She hunched over the meal and slowly began picking at it.

"Once, when I was little, my father had a rule—not to go outside after sunset. I always kept that rule because I trusted my father and loved him. But one night I thought that I heard a cat meowing. It sounded sad and scared. Daddy had already gone to bed, and I didn't see what the big deal would be if I went out and checked on it, at least gave it some food. So I filled a bowl with water and another with leftovers from dinner, and I took them outside.

"The meowing continued, and I followed it to a row of hedges that we had at our old house. I called for the cat, but it didn't answer. Just as I was putting the food and the bowl down, something leaped out and attacked me."

Paige's hands flew to her mouth. "No! What happened."

"I screamed, or I thought that I did. I screamed and cried, beating at the creature. It ripped into me, but I didn't feel it. Next thing I knew, the creature was gone and Daddy was standing beside me. He was holding me to his chest and running. He took me inside the house and used all his magic to mend me. Which he did."

"And the creature?" I asked.

She shook her head. "He wounded it. We never found it."

"But you were okay," Paige said.

"Yes, though I would've been eaten if it had taken Daddy any longer to arrive."

Matt sipped his tea. "Good thing that didn't happen."

"My point is"—she leaned over the table and held my gaze with her sharp eyes that sparkled with intelligence—"I didn't listen to my father and it almost got me killed. If I had trusted his instincts, trusted him, things would have gone a lot better. I never would have been attacked. So from that day forward, I've learned to listen to him, to trust. Because he knows best. It might seem like he's keeping things from you for nefarious reasons, but I can promise that's not the case. The truth is, he's doing it for your own good, because that's what's necessary. So just trust him. You've made it this far, haven't you?"

I'd made it this far, and I'd trusted Horatio only to be lied to by him. He was her father, so of course she trusted him. He'd saved her life. But he'd lied to me about the werewolf, and I couldn't help but wonder what else either he was lying about or not telling the whole truth on.

"You can't blame me for wondering," I said to her. "It's my life we're talking about."

"You've gotten the doses of the cure that you need. Just one more to go and you'll be completely healed. All you have to do is trust and everything will go smoothly."

Trust him. Those were two big words that I wasn't sure that I could do, but I didn't say anything else to Drea about it.

The rest of dinner was pretty quiet except for Matt, who asked Drea all kinds of questions about the area and her life. She answered, but the gloom of our earlier conversation hovered about the room like a third wheel on a date.

When we were finished, I helped Paige clean up while Matt escorted Drea into the living room so they could finish their discussion on the types of cheese he liked.

It was much too intriguing a conversation for me.

"Well, that went...not as good as I hoped." Paige handed me a dry plate, and I put it in the cupboard. "I was hoping she'd give up a teensy bit more information than nothing."

I smirked. "Now what fun would it have been if she'd told us what we wanted to know?"

"More fun than not knowing." Paige sighed. "I guess we'll just have to wait until tomorrow."

Perhaps. Or perhaps I'd find a way to break into that room downstairs, the one that Horatio kept locked up. Because for all the rooms in the house, there wasn't an office anywhere. That was strange. Why would a man like Horatio, one who clearly has a lot of paperwork and details to go over, not have an office in his house? He had a den. He had a bedroom, but not a spot where he did his work.

He had an office, and it had to be behind that door. What could be so secret that he'd keep it locked up, away from spying eyes, and all the way in the bowels of the house?

Something that was worth keeping a secret.

"Grim? What are you thinking? I see that mind of yours going, but you're not saying anything."

This I didn't want Paige to know. If Horatio was going to be mad at anyone, he could be angry at me, not her.

So I smiled tightly. "I'm not thinking about anything at all."

21

I'd have to work quickly, getting into that room before Horatio returned. After dinner I complained of being tired and headed to my room. But after a few minutes I sneaked back out. Voices came from the kitchen—Drea and Matt. There was no telling where Paige had gotten off to, and part of me felt guilty for not telling her what I was doing, but this was for her own safety.

At least that was what I kept telling myself.

I slipped downstairs and punched in the code that unlocked the basement door. Horatio hadn't made any attempt to hide it, so I'd made a point to remember earlier.

The lights buzzed when I flipped the switch. As I blinked against the sharpness of the light, my heart thundered against my chest.

There was no reason to worry. No one would be coming downstairs, not for any reason. I was all alone.

I stared at the metal patient table as I passed it, wondering if I'd have to be strapped down a third time when the final dose was administered.

With my luck I would be.

The door that was tucked way in the back of the room stared at me in challenge, as if it knew there was no way that I'd ever be able to crack it open.

I lifted my hand over the keypad, and a green light swept down the surface, looking for a handprint to scan.

There was no way I'd be able to get through the door without Horatio. I'd have to find another way to break in.

But…would it be possible to fool the technology? I threw a rewinding spell on the surface of the scanner, trying to get it to recall the last time the door was unlocked. It was no good. The door absorbed my spell like it was sucking it up through a straw.

Horatio would expect someone to attempt to break in magically. I had to outsmart him if I was going to get past that door.

I attempted a spell that would neutralize the electronics, but they held fast. He'd anticipated that someone would do that, too.

What did he have behind this door that was such a big secret? What was it?

And if I couldn't fool the keypad, how was I going to get past the thing?

"What are you doing?"

I nearly jumped out of my skin at the sound of Paige's voice. I whirled around as her foot touched the last step of the stairs. She scrunched up her face as if she'd walked through a bad smell.

"What are *you* doing here?" I threw at her.

"Looking for you. I knew you weren't tired. I just didn't know what you were up to."

"You should go back upstairs."

She dropped her voice to a whisper. "And miss you breaking into that room? No way."

THE WITHERING STORM

"I don't think I'll be able to. Horatio's got all kinds of shields on it. He's thought about every which way a person would want to break into it."

"Has he? Well, he is smart, but I bet you're smarter."

In that moment I wasn't feeling very smart.

Paige approached the keypad and stared at it. "Huh. Uses a handprint, I guess."

"So it would seem."

"And what all have you tried?"

I went through the list, which wasn't very long. When I finished, she smirked. "It's too bad I don't know more about magic. The best I can do is wish that somehow you could make Horatio's handprint appear. Like, what if you could lift it off one of those instruments over there."

My jaw dropped. "Or even lift it off the scanner itself. Paige, you're brilliant." I brushed my lips to her cheek. "If I can pull his handprint off the surface, we may be able to get somewhere. But I'll have to be careful."

She peered over my shoulder at the black panel. "Why's that?"

"Because I could set off the scanner and it would lock down, shutting us out and alerting Horatio that we've been tampering with it."

"Yikes. If you want to stay on his good side, maybe we should forget all about it." We stared at each other a beat before she shook her head. "Never mind. Forget I said that. So. How're you going to do this?"

How was I? I considered it a moment and snapped my fingers. "I need your help."

Her eyes glinted at the idea of challenge. "How can I help?"

"You have to siphon magic into me. I'm still weak and not at one hundred percent. This will drain you, though."

"Grim, you know I'd do anything for you."

My heart nearly burst from my chest at the emotion that

139

stirred in me. I closed my eyes and swallowed. Paige was…my everything. If I drained her and something happened…what if she needed her magic?

"Forget it. It's too dangerous."

"No." She grabbed my sleeve. "Don't push me away."

"There are risks."

"I'm willing to take them. Grim, you don't get to decide for me what's too dangerous. That's not fair."

"It is when I'm responsible for you. You wouldn't be here if it wasn't for me."

She rubbed her thumb across my cheek. "And I'm grateful that I am here. You need answers, and if I can help you get them, use me. You have to. Otherwise what's the point of us being here at all? Might as well turn around and go back upstairs."

She was right. I'd come this far; there was no backing down now. "Okay. But if you start to feel weak, tell me to stop and I will."

"Deal." Her gaze whipped around the room like she was searching for something. "What do you need me to do?"

"Stand beside me."

She came up and I pressed one hand to her shoulder. Magic jumped under her skin. She was full of power. It was more than what I needed.

I gently tugged on her magic, but it didn't want to come. So I pulled harder. Then magic flowed like I'd pushed a boulder out from under a mountain of rocks. It slammed into me, rocking me back on my heels.

Paige's eyes flared in surprise. "I wasn't expecting…that."

"That should have been the worst of it. Hold steady."

It took several seconds, but I finally got control of the speed and amount of magic that I needed. I slowed the velocity to a trickle and pushed against it so that I wouldn't take too much.

THE WITHERING STORM

The scared look on her face melted off, and it was when she looked relaxed and calm that I focused on the panel.

I channeled my magic and sent light strands of gossamer-like electrical particles onto the surface. I laid them down in layers, building them up one strand at a time.

It was grueling work. If I put down too many layers at once, the panel would short-circuit and the jig would be up.

It was also tiring taking Paige's power. I had to focus on that, making sure that I wasn't pulling too much from her, while at the same time building up those strands.

After about ten minutes, an image finally appeared.

"His hand," Paige murmured.

It was indeed a hand—Horatio's. The fine lines of his prints were slowly forming. Just a few more minutes and I'd have what I needed.

"How're you doing?" I asked her.

She gave me a feeble smile. "Hanging in there."

I'd taken more magic than I should have. "Almost done."

"No rush," she said through a yawn.

The last bits of the print appeared, and I sighed in relief. Finally, now all that was needed was to pull it off.

I dropped my hand from Paige's shoulder, and she rocked back. I snaked my arm around her waist and caught her.

"You okay?"

"Fine. I'll be fine."

I frowned. "Let me take you upstairs."

"No." She waved off my concern. "You're almost done. Let's see what's behind the door."

She was tired. Very tired. She shouldn't have been here. Paige needed to be in bed, collecting her strength. "You sure?"

"Of course. I haven't come this far, Grim, to not see what Horatio's hiding."

"If you're sure."

She gave me a huge grin. "I'm sure. Now hurry up."

AMY BOYLES

Against my better judgment, I released my grip from around her waist and studied the print. It was perfect. Completely formed.

I slipped my hand into the 3-D image of Horatio's, one constructed of electricity as it tingled against my skin. I sent one last bit of spell into the hand, and it tightened against my skin, becoming a waxy outer layer.

It was exactly what I needed.

"Here goes nothing," I mumbled as I pressed my hand to the scanner.

The green line swept up and down, reading the print. Sweat sprinkled my brow as I waited for what seemed like an eternity before the scanner beeped and a click sounded from the door.

"We're in."

Six inches of reinforced steel slowly swung outward. I opened it wide enough for the both of us to step inside. Once in, I flipped on a light and shut the door behind us.

More buzzing lights flickered to life. This room was much smaller than the last one, and it was as I suspected—it housed Horatio's office.

A desk sat atop a bloodred Oriental rug. Built-in wooden shelves were placed behind it, showcasing objects that Horatio had collected in his days of monster hunting.

That was all this was—an office.

"Huh," said Paige.

Huh, indeed.

"I was expecting more oomph," she said.

"I was, too."

If this was his office, why was it so protected? I threw out the little bit of magic that I had left toward his desk, but didn't find any spells that were meant to conceal. There were filing cabinets behind his desk, but I had a feeling all I would see in those were financials. Nothing that I was interested in.

So then why was this place hidden?

Paige patted my shoulder. "I'm going back up."

"You need to lie down. If you wait a minute, I'll close up and join you."

She shook her head. "No, no. I'll see you upstairs."

Without another word, she left while I was still trying to figure out why this place was so important.

The collectibles on his shelves looked to be more personal than valuable. There was something that I had to be missing.

But what?

My gaze swept over the desk and the shelves again before I decided that Paige was right—there wasn't anything here, at least nothing that was worth me snooping around for.

I grabbed the door and was halfway through it when it hit me.

Another spell.

It hovered in the air lightly, as if it barely existed, but it did exist, and I felt it.

A concealment spell.

The hair on the back of my neck lifted to attention as I turned back around. I stared at the far wall, and that was when I saw the shimmery cast of power.

The magic was so well done, so delicately laid and layered, that Horatio wanted it to be missed.

He *was* hiding something.

I knew it.

With the little bit of magic I had left, I lifted my hand and waved it over the wall. The power that hid whatever it was that Horatio found important enough to secret away, shimmered and vibrated before it melted.

The wall that had sat on one side of the room vanished, and when I blinked—because I had to blink half a dozen times to make sure that what I was seeing correctly wasn't a mirage —a secret laboratory appeared.

But this wasn't a regular laboratory. This lab was full of specimens—monster specimens.

And they were alive.

22

It felt like I was in a dystopian movie where a scientific genius had been collecting creature specimens for years and was keeping them alive for his pleasure alone.

Glass cases filled the room, and inside those cases were dozens of monsters—more species than I imagined that could fit inside the room.

The first I spotted was a large aquarium that held water sprites living in an artificial creek setting.

The sprites hissed at me with daggerlike teeth as I passed. They were more pesky than dangerous. But those were the gentlest of what was before me.

The Tazmanian Prowler, a fierce beast about the size of a Great Dane with long claws and a mouth that opened as wide as a hippopotamus's, roared at me. It smashed its head against the glass, infuriated by my presence.

Beyond that were dozens of monsters—some more humanlike and others resembling beasts.

They were all alive and staring at me as if they wanted to eat me for dinner.

"What in the world?"

Horatio had spent his entire life capturing and keeping these monsters—dangerous beasts that would eat you as soon as look at you, and that was obvious by the terrible claws and pieces of meat hanging in some of the creature's mouths. He'd taken them and created some sort of strange zoo.

But that wasn't all of it. A table ran the length of the room. Clusters of test tubes sat in slotted racks. They were filled with blood. On closer inspection, the vials were marked.

"Prowler specimen, tree beast, hybrid."

Hybrid? I worked my way through the maze of creatures, heading deeper into the fold. There were monsters that I recognized, many of them. But I'd overlooked the back area— where creatures the likes of which the world had never seen— mashups between Long-tailed Earth Tubers (worms as big as a horse) mixed with Short-snouted Wombles (bat-looking creatures). And there were more.

More hybrids of things that shouldn't have existed. Horatio had spliced cold-blooded monsters with invertebrates, warm-blooded furry creatures with insect-like beasts. The combinations were not only disconcerting, they were also disastrous. Creatures that should have had legs, instead only possessed bodies to slither around on. Blind monsters wound up with extra sharp sight, and so on.

It was disgusting, these abominations. The combinations and collection overwhelmed me. My dinner surged up from my stomach and deposited itself on the floor.

What Horatio had done wasn't simply illegal. It was monstrous. None of these creatures should have existed. They weren't created in nature, but Horatio had determined that they should have lived.

This was too much. Cure or no cure, I had to get out of here. The council needed to know about this. Carrington Dorn would forget all about wanting to arrest me. He'd have

THE WITHERING STORM

much bigger fish to fry with Horatio. The medal that the council would give Dorn for bringing Horatio to justice would inflate his head for the rest of his life.

He might even thank me for the tip-off.

Then again, he probably wouldn't.

With my stomach still churning, I slowly made my way back through the menagerie, mentally noting all the hybrids and wondering just exactly how Horatio had managed to become such a sicko.

Was it the monster hunting that had done this to him? What would cause a person to want to play Dr. Frankenstein? What drove a person to that extreme?

I didn't know and didn't care. All I wanted to do was get Paige and Matt and leave this place as quickly as possible.

As I made my way through the mess of monsters, my gaze snagged on an empty case. This was human sized and looked to be more like a stasis holder, the sort of thing that you'd see filled with water, the creature inside asleep, with tubes running from its body to some unseen apparatus that fed it oxygen and kept it alive.

What was he saving that case for?

I shouldn't have looked. Even as I approached the cylinder, a knot erupted in my stomach, telling me to run, to leave the lab as quickly as my feet would take me.

Don't look! Run!

But curiosity got the better of me, so I moved in, noting that the case was brand-new, looking as if it had just been installed. The concrete surrounding it was freshly poured to secure it to the room.

I leaned in and read the brass plaque at the bottom.

WITHERING.

My blood turned to ice, and my heart stopped beating. A case for a withering.

The case was for me. I was the only withering around,

AMY BOYLES

unless Horatio planned to capture one of the witherings that seemed to pop up simply because of my presence.

Somehow I doubted it.

Leave. Now.

I had to get out of this place.

I raced through the room, coming out on the other side, into Horatio's office with my chest heaving as if I'd just run a marathon.

Adrenaline was pouring into my veins, but I knew that as soon as it wore off, I'd be exhausted and would need to rest.

So I had to leave, and quickly.

Inside of Horatio's actual office, I threw up my hand, restoring the magical barrier. Then I made my way through the thick door and out into the basement.

Upstairs, I raced to Paige's room, but it was empty.

I found Matt in his, scrolling on a tablet. "We're leaving. Pack up."

His head snapped up. "What are you talking about?"

"Right now. Where's Paige?"

His jaw dropped in confusion. "I think she went outside. I heard the back door open."

Outside, where there had been a bowl that Horatio told me didn't exist, feeding a monster that he had also claimed didn't exist.

Oh God.

Horatio was trying to catch that werewolf.

"There's no time to explain. We need to find her and—"

But I was cut off, because from outside I heard Paige— screaming.

23

$\mathcal{M}$ore adrenaline pumped through my body as I charged through the house.

The sound of Matt's pounding feet was right behind me. "Sounded like it came from the back."

I agreed. We raced downstairs and out the back door.

I was not prepared for what I saw next.

Paige was pressed up against a tree, trembling. Holding her in place was the werewolf.

"Let her go," I snarled.

The creature swung its head and glared at me with yellow eyes.

"I say we just hit it with magic," Matt whispered. "Forget about niceties."

He had a good point. The problem was that my magic was nearly depleted.

A yelp slipped from Paige's mouth, and the monster turned its focus back onto her. It reared its head and looked half a second away from biting into her neck.

I didn't wait. I threw every bit of magic that I had left at the beast. Matt did the same. His power was stronger, and without him I doubt that I would've been able to fight the creature off.

The beast fell to the ground. As soon as we stopped hitting it with power, it turned its attention to us.

Now it was angry.

But at least it was leaving Paige alone.

"Matt, get her inside."

"What? No. You need my help."

"I need you both inside, now," I snapped.

He didn't argue. Paige rushed over to him, and I assumed that Matt grabbed her. I didn't know because I wasn't taking my eyes off the creature that was slowly stalking toward me.

"You want to destroy that child. You want to destroy Paige. Why is Horatio feeding you?"

The creature's lips pulled back. "You don't listen," it said in a low, raspy voice.

Wow. It talked. And I'd thought it was just a mindless creature chained to its curse. "I hadn't really expected you to answer."

"But yet I did. You don't listen, Grim. You poke your nose in places where it shouldn't belong."

I cocked my head. How could this creature know that?

"I know a lot of things," it hissed, its voice now sounding snakelike. "I know a lot about you and how you think that you're untouchable. You're not untouchable."

While it spoke, I'd been letting my power churn inside of me. It was building up, ready to be released in one powerful blow. I had one shot at this, and I needed to get it right.

"I'm not untouchable," I argued. "But neither are you."

"Now you die."

The creature pounced, and I hit it with every bit of magic that I possessed. But my power didn't touch it. I was tapped out. The beast dodged my blows and landed on me, knocking me to the ground.

I still had my strength. Before it could bite, I flung it off and rolled on top of it. I pressed my hand to its chest, right where its heart was. It thrashed and snapped. With my free hand, I pushed its face to one side as I straddled it.

It wouldn't take much magic to end the beast's life. Just the right amount to the heart and the creature would be done for.

Magic swirled under my palm. The hot glow of power illuminated my skin. Just one more second and this would be over.

"Step away from the wolf," came Horatio's voice.

The creature immediately stopped thrashing. Standing just outside the door with two pistols, one pointed at Paige and the other at Matt, was Horatio.

"I said, put your hand down and step away from the wolf."

As I wasn't in any position to argue, I did as he said and slowly climbed off the beast.

"Drea, come here." The wolf flipped over and padded to Horatio. "Now, now," he scolded. "Be nice to our guests. I told you that you couldn't eat them, remember?"

As the wolf/beast padded over to Horatio, it slowly changed form, becoming human and eventually standing on two feet.

Horatio threw a cloak at Drea, who wrapped it over her shoulders. "But they've been snooping," Drea said.

He nodded. "I know."

I wasn't sure which was more shocking—that Drea was the werewolf creature or that they knew we'd been snooping.

"I smelled it on her," Drea said, cocking her head at Paige.

Ah, her canine sense of smell had betrayed us. Well, if I'd known that she was the werewolf, I would have countered for that.

"So she's existed all this time," I said bitterly.

"She has, but she was none of your concern," he said primly. "Now, why don't we all go inside and have a nice chat?

Come along. You first, Grim, and don't even think of trying anything, because if you do, they'll die. I will shoot them both at once. So be good, won't you?"

As I didn't want my friend and my girlfriend to die, it appeared that I'd be minding my p's and q's—at least for now.

When we were all inside, Drea disappeared for a moment and returned dressed in a tracksuit. "Tea?"

"Yes, Drea, that would be perfect."

Horatio gestured with the gun for me to sit at the dining table. Paige and Matt did the same. Our celebrity host took the head, while the three of us sat in empty chairs down from him. His aim on Paige and Matt didn't waiver for a second as we waited in silence for Drea to make the tea and then serve it.

"Thank you." Horatio let the tea cool for a moment while watching us with eyes glittering with malice. "Feel free to drink at any time."

"I've lost my appetite," Paige snarled.

"My dear, I can understand, but you have no one to blame but yourself. Drea said that you've been snooping."

"The lab," his daughter snitched.

Horatio's jaw fell. "Well, well, well, it appears that I underestimated your talents, Grim. How'd you do it? Unless it was you, Matt, but I highly doubt it. You don't seem the type who has any interest in snooping, and it certainly wasn't Paige. She hasn't had her magic long enough to know how to circumvent electronics."

"It was her idea," I told him.

"Color me shocked." He leaned forward, eyes hard. "But tell me, how'd you get in? I must know as I'll have to fix whatever bug you worked your way around."

Keeping the information from Horatio could set him off and make him more likely to shoot someone. So I told him. "I

THE WITHERING STORM

created a sleeve with your handprint, pulling it off the panel with magic."

"Ingenious. I'll have to find a way to keep someone else from being able to do that. How very, very clever. I have to give you credit. I didn't think you'd be able to do something like that, much less walk through my office and see the rest of it."

"The rest of what?" Matt asked.

Silence until Horatio finally dragged his gaze from me to focus on Matt. "Though I'm tempted to let your friend explain it, I'm afraid that he'll botch the whole thing and make it look more dramatic than what it really is.

"It all started when Drea was a girl. One night she went outside, even though I'd told her not to. Sound familiar to anyone?" His gaze darted to me before he turned back to Matt. "While she was out there, my daughter was attacked."

"By a monster, we know," Matt finished for him.

"Ah ah, not just any monster. Would anyone like to take a guess at what got her?"

"A werewolf," Paige murmured.

"Correct!" Horatio placed one of the guns on the table in front of him and sipped his tea. When he finished the drink, he picked the pistol back up, aiming it again at Paige. "I heard her scream and found her—but not until after the werewolf had already bit her, transferring the virus that lived inside of it to my daughter."

Matt frowned. "Couldn't you track down the beast and kill it? Would that end the curse?"

"That only works in movies. It's no wonder you're not a monster hunter. You don't know anything about these things."

"I never pretended to."

"As I can see." Horatio inhaled deeply, refocusing. "Anyway, I did kill the creature, but the damage was already done. Drea was infected. What was I to do? What could I do? I was a monster hunter. I couldn't have my own child be a monster as well. They'd take her away from me. She'd be destroyed. So that began my search for a cure. At first I collected herbs and plants, creating combinations of cures that I thought might be able to help. But nothing worked. Then I realized that maybe the cure wasn't in a plant. Perhaps it could be found in another monster. Certain monsters follow the same bloodlines. Maybe there was something in the blood that would help me."

"So you started collecting specimens," I said, disgusted.

"Yes. This was for science, Grim. You have to understand that. If I could find a breakthrough, something that would end a werewolf's curse, how many lives would that save? How many people would we be able to help? This was important work."

Work that eventually went wrong. But I kept that to myself.

"So the experiments began. I collected samples. I gave them to Drea. Before this started, she couldn't control herself. She would transform on a full moon, but I'd have to chain her up. She was feral. With the help of my research, she changed." His face brightened. "No longer was she some mindless beast. She was able to think, and we were able to change her very nature. Now she can control when she shifts, and those primal instincts are almost nonexistent."

"Nonexistent?" I spat. "How can you call slaughtering sheep and wanting to break into a little boy's room to devour him 'nonexistent'?"

A muscle in Horatio's jaw pulsed. "Those things will eventually go away."

"No, they won't," I argued quietly. "You can't cure her of what she is—a werewolf."

THE WITHERING STORM

"Just like I can't cure you of becoming a withering?"

The room stilled and we stared at one another. Finally, after a long pause, I said, "Maybe you can't. Maybe there's no way to actually heal me, and you wouldn't know that anyway, would you? Because your story of being turned into one is false, right?"

He stared at me for a long moment before a slow smile crept across his face. "And here I thought that I'd done such a great job convincing you that I'd once been in your shoes. I even put a fake scar on my arm."

"I was convinced, for a long time I was, until tonight."

Matt's head swiveled from me to Horatio and back. "What changed? What happened?"

"It appears that our supersleuth Grim has seen what he wasn't supposed to. Not only has he seen my experiments—"

"You call those experiments? Creating mutants of monsters, abominations that shouldn't exist? Those creatures are in pain. Half of them can't move. They're not supposed to exist."

"What I do, I do for science!" Horatio pounded a fist on the table. I stared at the gun, exhaling a breath in thanks that it hadn't gone off. I couldn't keep pressing Horatio. Make him too angry and he would shoot someone.

And with my luck, it *wouldn't* be me.

He stopped puffing out his red cheeks and exhaled. "What I'm doing is hard for many to understand. This is experimental science, but what is science if not an experiment? What I've been able to do for Drea has been nothing short of miraculous."

"But what of the creatures?" I asked calmly. "What about what's best for them?"

His eyes narrowed. "These are monsters, Grim. Monsters that would eat you in a moment. Have you forgotten that? Did

155

that escape your mind? You of all people should know that you're nothing but a meal to them, nothing but blood and bones."

"And you're keeping them alive. Drea will kill Raja if she's given the chance. She'll kill anything because it is in her bones. It is in her DNA."

The look in his eyes became wild. "It's what's in your DNA now, too, Grim. Don't forget that."

How could I? Though the fire and anger in me had been dormant these past few days, seeing Drea holding Paige and talking to Horatio about all of this was churning up emotions inside of me. It was making the fury that I'd buried deep down rise back up.

"Tell me, Horatio. Where'd you get the first heart that you fed me?"

His face paled. "Be careful what questions you ask. You may not like the answer."

"You killed the witch."

He tipped his head from side to side. "I did track down a witch who knew how to cure the withering infection. She told me everything that I needed to know, from beginning to end. The only portion of your cure that I lied to you about is the hallucinations, and that was a necessary lie. Wasn't it? But it didn't work."

"It didn't work because I saw through it. I saw through you, Horatio."

He smirked. "We all have our masks."

I folded my arms. "So what do we do now?"

"Now, my dear Grim, we continue as we had planned. We shoot our last live show. You'll be given the final cure."

"What is it?"

"Now, now. That would ruin the fun. Can't have that, can we? There are some things that are left as a surprise. Now. Let's get set up."

THE WITHERING STORM

He rose and walked over to me, keeping one gun trained on Paige. "As much as I'd love for you to see what happens next, I'm afraid it'll be best if you're knocked out for this."

Before I could say a word, Horatio slammed the butt of the gun onto my head and everything went black.

24

I dreamed that I was standing on the beach, staring out at the ocean. Wind ripped through my hair, and waves crested and pounded the sand.

"You look happy."

Paige was beside me, her hair riding the wind's current. She smiled at me, and it was like watching dawn break. There wasn't anything that I wouldn't do for this woman, no man I wouldn't beat aside, and no mountain that I wouldn't climb for her. She was my everything.

"I am happy," I told her.

"Good. Because the games are about to begin."

"The games?"

She tipped her head back and laughed maniacally. The sound wasn't her own. It belonged to another person.

"Get ready, Grim," she said in a deep voice. "The games are beginning, and we'll see if you die."

My heart twisted in pain as Paige continued to laugh before she melted away and was replaced by Horatio Crooks.

My eyes popped open. I was outside, lying on something.

THE WITHERING STORM

The night was pitch-black except for bright lights shining on me. I attempted to lift my hand to shield my eyes.

My arm was tied down. Both of them were.

"Paige?"

A muffled cry came from my left. I squinted past the light and was able to make out Paige and Matt. They were tied to chairs and hanging from a tree.

The rope that secured them was wound around a massive oak.

The only thing missing from this scenario was a swinging scythe slowly lowering to fray and cut the rope, sending them crashing to their deaths.

"Can't have them distracting you, now can I?"

Horatio popped into view like a leprechaun, grinning from ear to ear. "Are you ready, Grim? It's almost showtime."

"Two minutes until we're live," Drea told him from behind the lights and the camera that were set up.

I could see everything now. My eyes had finally adjusted to the brightness.

"Why am I tied?" I snarled.

"I don't need you running away, not when we're so close to having everything. I assume that you saw the spot I cleared out for you in my lab? You don't have to answer because I know you did. Well, this is where you complete your destiny so that I can keep you there. Will you be dead or alive when it's all said and done? How will you wind up becoming part of my collection? Because rest assured, you will become part of it. One way or another. But let's see what happens, yes? Let's see what the viewers want."

"Ten seconds," Drea called.

Horatio smiled. "It's showtime. Smile for the camera."

"And five, four..."

She lifted her hand and counted down the last three

AMY BOYLES

seconds on her fingers. When the red light on top of the camera came on, Horatio was all smiles.

The smile of a madman.

Uncle Geezer was going to hear from me about sending in Horatio Crooks.

"Welcome, ladies and gentlemen. It's a beautiful night for the final episode of Grim's tale. So glad that all of you could join us. We're here with Grim, and it's the last time we'll be with him, because after tonight he will either be healed or he won't." His eyes flashed on me. "How're you doing, Grim?"

"If anyone—"

Horatio cocked his head toward Paige and Matt, a silent warning telling me to keep my mouth closed or else they'd suffer the consequences.

I glared at him with as much hate as I could muster.

Horatio asked his question again. "How are you, Grim?"

"Fine," I said through clenched teeth.

"Are you ready for what's going to happen? For the conclusion? The end that you've been waiting for?"

"Yes."

He whipped his head toward the camera. "Ladies and gentlemen, Grim doesn't know what's about to happen. He's been good on this journey with us, riding the waves of surprise with gusto. But tonight is the biggest wave yet. It's the wave that you and he have been holding your breaths for. It's all come down to this moment. So, is everyone at home ready? How about we take a vote? If you want to see what happens next, text 'yes' to the number on your screen. We'll give that a few seconds. In the meantime, let's talk to Grim."

He stalked to me and bent over. "Comfortable?"

"As much as I can be."

"What are you expecting tonight?"

A thousand replies fired off in my head, but most of them would get someone killed. "I'm not sure what to expect."

THE WITHERING STORM

"Doesn't that make this fun? Isn't that the best part?"

"I suppose."

He asked me mundane questions for a few more seconds before he turned away and picked up his tablet, talking again to the audience to fill time while all the replies filtered in.

I took the opportunity to inspect how I was tied down. Horatio had used metal cuffs. Just my luck. No knots that could be undone. The only possible means of escape was to use magic, and Horatio would be expecting that, so he would have made sure my magic couldn't break them.

My gaze flitted up to Matt and Paige. Perhaps a better plan was to free them. But with the seconds that it would take to lower and unbind them, by the time they were free and on the ground, Horatio and Drea would be thrown into action. But what would those two do on camera? They wouldn't kill anyone on camera.

Would they?

Even though Horatio was completely unhinged, he wasn't about to let his career suffer. His celebrity was as much of his identity as any other part of him. He'd been famous too long to let go of it.

"It appears the results are in," Horatio announced. "Grim, everyone wants to see what happens next. I knew they would. We all want to, don't we. Are you ready?"

For what? But what choice did I have except to say, "Yes."

"Very well. Grim, meet your destiny."

Horatio snapped his fingers, and a blink later, he was gone. They were all gone. All of them, and I was no longer strapped to the metal bed.

But I was in the exact same place, or so it seemed. The house was down from me, the tree that Paige and Matt were hanging from was not far off. Everything was the same except I was the only person around.

It was some sort of trick. I knew that. They had to still be here; it was just that I couldn't see any of them.

"Grim," Horatio's voice boomed from everywhere and nowhere at the same time, *"there was never a cure. Everything that you've done, everything that you've taken—none of it helped you. I used my magic to make it look like you were healing, to make you feel better, but there was never any hope for you. Now. Let's reveal what you really look like."*

His words were a sledgehammer to the gut. Never a cure? It was all a lie?

Why was I surprised?

The glamour he'd had on me faded, and the inky darkness that had been overtaking my body had grown like a vine all over me. My body was corroding, literally from the inside out. I was overcome with scarred tissue.

It was only a matter of minutes, hours before I was completely overtaken.

Next thing I knew, the ground began to shake as if an earthquake was ripping the earth apart.

I waited, because there was no place to go, no need to run.

And that was when I saw them. Three witherings approached, walking slowly, their very presence sucking the goodness from the world.

They looked like large stalks of corn with eyes like coal briquettes and arms that were long, with roped muscles.

Horatio had magicked himself and everyone else invisible. Would the withering still see them? Sense them?

He was playing with fire here.

And he knew exactly what he was doing. Because if the withering sensed my friends, they'd attack them. They'd do the same thing to them that had been done to me. So I had to make sure that never came to fruition.

They stopped when they were a few yards away and

studied me. The tallest one, who was about as tall as a small crepe myrtle tree, spoke.

You have denied us.

"I have denied what you want me to be. I won't become you. My heart won't shrivel into a stone like yours."

He lifted his head and silently laughed. *You think there's a choice.*

"Of course there's a choice."

Come with us and become your destiny.

He lifted his hand, and magic shot into me. It felt like my chest was being ripped open. Pain and suffering bubbled under my skin. It invaded my mind. Its claws hooked into me and dragged me to it.

Anger and the desire to destroy, to be the only living thing in the world, was overwhelming.

And that was when, for the first time, I understood the withering.

This creature, one who was such legend, who few had ever encountered, told me its story.

I saw a man wearing rags being thrown from his village, stoned out, until he ran into the desert. The sun was so hot, so strong that he would die if he didn't find shelter.

At last an enclosure came into view. He was so tired, so very, very tired, and he was angry, furious at the villagers who'd cast him out.

He was a criminal, a bad man, one who took advantage of anyone he could—killing, stealing.

He'd gotten what he deserved.

He wandered into the cave and rested, waiting out the sun. When nighttime came, he made a fire using sticks and dried grass. He was hungry, so he thought there might be a rodent or maybe a snake in the cave.

He made a torch and walked into it. The cave led him

down, where the air became cooler. Finally he saw a pool of water.

A mirage, he thought, though he knew that mirages only occurred during the day, when the sun hit the sand so that it shimmered like water.

This was no mirage.

He moved to drink it, but the pool had a guardian. A giant cobra that lifted its head and flicked its tongue in warning.

Drink from this pool, the snake told him, *and your descendants will forever be cursed. You will be cursed. You will cease to become a man, and you will only become the worst of yourself. Whoever you touch will also become like you.*

The man didn't care. All he wanted to do was drink. So he did. He lapped at the water like a dog. The moment the water touched his tongue, the snake disappeared.

Must have been his imagination the whole time.

At first he felt fine. But within hours he wasn't. His body was on fire; he knew he was going to die. Whatever had been in that water was going to kill him.

He spent the night thrashing, waiting for death to take him.

But it did not.

It changed him. His skin changed—it became both papery and sinewy at the same time. His body grew. He was tall like a giant. And his heart hardened.

The heart that was already cold and stony to mankind became an impenetrable block of slate. He hated his village for what they had done to him. They needed to pay.

So that night he left the cave and returned to the village. He slaughtered every person he could find. It didn't matter who they were. He didn't stop killing until he was done.

And he felt satisfied.

But all that work took a toll on him. He became tired, so he

THE WITHERING STORM

walked until he found a place deep in another cave, one abandoned, and he slept.

He slept for so long that when he finally woke up, things
had changed. The world looked different.

And he was lonely.

So he closed his eyes and he searched until he felt another
heart as black as his. He tracked that heart, looking for that
person until he found him.

And he turned that person into someone just like him.

But the light, he found, hurt his eyes. It hurt his body. He
had to keep to the darkness, where he wasn't in pain. He also
found that he slept for a long time, but when he did awaken,
he was usually angry, frustrated and wanting to hurt others.

He wanted to hurt others like he had been hurt, because
from what he remembered of his life before he became new
(and it wasn't much), but what he recalled was that there was
much pain and suffering. People hurt him. People he trusted
and loved.

So he wanted to hurt everyone and everything possible. So
he and the other hurt more people as they journeyed to a land
where no one would find them.

People tried to hurt them back, but they couldn't be
touched. The snake had lied to him. It hadn't said that now he
couldn't be harmed. The snake had made his life seem terrible.
But this was truly living. It was the first time that the man,
now a creature, felt alive, felt free.

And on it went until now, when he stood in front of a man
who had refused to come into the fold, had refused to become
one of them. Perhaps it was because this man was too good.
He didn't have a black heart like the others. He was turned
because of fate instead of being turned because he would
embrace his destiny.

Who was this creature who was no more important than

an ant, that he had called the withering from his deep slumber to deal with the problem himself?

He had lived a long time and had brought many into his fold. Why was this one puny man resisting what was glorious?

So he showed him everything, showed him the power that would be at his fingertips, showed him how the real condition of the heart is not suffering but embracing the strength that suffering led to.

You will be strong. You will have no fear. You will have no disease. You will become what you are to be.

The images, as quickly as they charged into my mind, faded. I knew what lay on the other side of acceptance. Horatio would do his best to take me. He would do everything that he could to grab me and make me his own.

I couldn't allow that any more than I could allow what Horatio would do to Paige and Matt. The TV star wouldn't allow them to live after everything that they'd seen. He'd come up with a story, something that was horrific and dramatic, to explain their deaths.

They tried to stop Grim from turning, he'd tell people. *But in the end Grim destroyed them. Don't worry, I was able to destroy him. There's no body because I had to burn it.*

And people would believe it.

They would believe any and every lie that fell from Horatio's lips. They'd gobble up those lies without question.

But I knew that Horatio would do everything in his power to stop me from walking away, and truth be told, the burning ache in my chest, the anger that lurked deep inside me—it was bubbling under my skin.

I couldn't, in my current condition, defeat Horatio.

I looked down at my chest. My shirt covered most of my torso, but just above the collar, the dark, inky pattern of infection was writhing on my flesh.

And it was stronger than before.

Come join us, he told me.

"No," I said. "You may take my body, but you'll never take my mind."

So be it.

The two creatures at the withering's sides rushed forward. They would kill me.

Anger flowed like adrenaline through my veins. A sudden spurt of power rushed into my arms and I pulled my wrists, breaking the cuffs that tied me to the bed.

The witherings moved fast, each of them striking out. In a flash, I was up and both blows until one got a hit in on my back.

The impact was so hard it felt like my spine had been broken in half. I doubled over and took a fist to the face with such force that I was flipped onto my back.

The old withering approached. *You cannot win.*

And I saw for the first time that he was right. I couldn't win. If I was going to defeat these creatures, then it would have to be done a different way, because I was no match for three of them.

The creature leaned in so close that I could make out every withered line in its corn-husk face. *This will hurt.*

I assumed it would.

He touched my chest with a glowing hand, and it felt like my body was turning into lava. I screamed in agony as my body was ripped apart, as my legs grew, as my arms grew, as I was transformed into a withering.

I don't know how long it took, but the pain seemed to stretch until forever, until it didn't. That was when the strength overtook me. My arms felt like tree trunks that could rip down a mountain. My legs felt like they could kick a thousand-pound weight across the ocean.

I was stronger than I ever imagined I could be.

I was a withering.

25

I looked down at my hands. They were the same as the other creatures'—sinewy with golden strips of withered husks.

Come join us. Feel the hatred and anger in your heart, he told me.

It was there, just waiting to burst open. There was so much anger inside. I wanted to destroy people, anything. Sinking into the mire of my mind would be so easy.

They would take me with them, these witherings, and we would harm and kill without remorse. My humanness was already gone. Why not let it go even more?

They had already taken my human body, why not let them take my human soul?

I will come, I said back in my mind, as there was no use for words now.

As soon as I rose, I reached out and hit the creature closest to me in the chest. The monster disintegrated before my eyes.

The leader whirled around, saw what had happened, and its face twisted in anger.

THE WITHERING STORM

But it was too late. I had already hit the withering on my left, turning it into dust.

You are supposed to be one of us, the leader roared.

I glared at the thing that had once been a human and had lived for centuries as a monster. *I will never be one of you.*

It attacked, reaching for me, getting ahold of my chest. I knocked its hand away and struck, grabbing it by the shoulder and throwing it back until it hit the ground.

The force of the impact made the earth tremble. Lights blinked behind me. I dared a look over my shoulder and spotted Horatio and the others.

His magic…it must've run out.

The withering rose and reached me with a speed that I didn't expect. I was struck in the chest before I could blink. The thing's hand was deep in my sternum, and it was grabbing my heart to destroy me.

No.

I couldn't let it win. Not like this.

I roared in pain and rear back my hand. I pushed it through the creature, elongating my arm in a way that was inhuman.

The monster's face morphed into surprise, and for a brief moment it looked down before the creature collapsed into a pile of dust.

But I was still ruined. The withering had gotten to my heart, and I didn't have much time.

With all my remaining strength I turned to Horatio, whose eyes were big as plates.

"No, audience," he yelled. "We've lost Grim. He's become the creature that we hoped he wouldn't. The rest of this you cannot see on television. We must cut the broadcast." The camera's light went off. "I'm sorry it's come to this, Grim. I thought for sure you'd win against them."

He would not be victorious.

I whipped out my arm. It stretched to the tree that Matt and Paige were hanging from. With one lash of my hand the rope cut, and with my other, stretching it as far as it would go, I lowered them to safety and sliced through the ropes holding them.

Horatio fumed. "You cannot!"

I whipped my hand out and knocked him into a tree, using my own corn husks to strap him down.

Drea tried to run, but I caught her and slapped her against a tree as well.

Paige raced to me, but there was no more strength in my body. I collapsed to the ground.

"Grim, no!" She came to a skidding stop on her knees and cradled my head. "No, no!"

"Dorn...Carrington..."

She looked over her shoulder. "Matt will call him now. We'll get him out here. Hold on, Grim. We'll save you. Hold on."

I took her hand and looked into her eyes that leaked tears. I had to force the next words out. The pain from where the withering had hit me was overtaking me now. Had to hold on for a few more seconds. "You...have...been the best...part of my life."

"No, Grim. Hang on. Don't go."

She didn't understand. I couldn't live like this, like a monster. Eventually the desire to destroy would overtake me. I wouldn't be able to control it. It was best for me to die.

As she cried and held me, I reached up and touched her hair one last time. "I love you."

She said the same thing as my eyes closed and I slipped away.

26

*D*arkness consumed everything. It was pitch-black, and then a light came. It dazzled as it spiraled toward me, eating up the inky black.

Two figures stood off in the distance. They approached slowly, smiles on their faces.

It took a moment before it sank in who I was looking at. "Mom? Dad?"

"Son," my dad said, opening his arms.

He looked exactly as he had in life—glasses on, wearing thick khaki pants that were perfect for hunting. His dark hair was cut short, his olive skin a stark contrast to his bright white teeth.

My mother smiled warmly. She was also the same—a little more round than my dad, but in that good, motherly way. She reached out and touched my hair.

"You've grown into a good man."

"A great man," Dad echoed as he hugged me.

They smelled like our old house, cozy and smoky from the fireplace. Their touch was real—it felt like I was with them.

"We're so proud of you," Mom said, pulling away from a hug.

"You've become more than we ever expected," Dad added. "You have helped so many people, and you stopped those creatures."

"No, I didn't. There are more of them in the world."

"There are more, but no longer," Mom told me. She fluffed the ends of her hair and beamed up at me. "Look at how big you've gotten. I almost didn't recognize you."

Wait. We needed to go back. "I stopped them?"

A concrete bench appeared, and my father led us over to it. As soon as we sat, he explained. "There was a curse on all the witherings that he had created. When the first died, that curse was lifted."

"But I was able to still be a monster."

"Only for a short while," Mom said, smoothing my hair in a way she used to do when I was a child and upset. "Breaking a spell can take time. It's not instantaneous like it is in the movies. You know that."

I did know that. I'd forgotten. This also meant that the withering I'd trapped in a book weeks ago, the one who'd infected me, was now human again. "So all the people that were turned, they've been set free?"

"Mm hm." Dad adjusted his glasses, pushing them up his nose with one finger. "Those that had already lived out their natural lives have gone on to the other side. Any who were turned recently would become human again."

"And what about what they've done? Dad, the evil that is within the withering heart"—I rubbed my eyes with the heels of my hands—"it's not anything that a person can escape."

"You did," my mother pointed out.

"But I wasn't one for long, and now I'm…dead. I suppose."

My parents exchanged a look. My mom spoke first. "You've been so good in life, Son. You've worked so hard to help people. You've hunted monsters and protected the innocent."

"Just like we taught you."

That was when the wall of guilt hit me. "But it's because of me...that you both died."

"No, shh, don't say things like that."

Dad shook his head. "You aren't responsible for our deaths. They were not your fault. The monster that tricked you would have found a way to kill us somehow, or to at least harm us. Never, not once have we blamed you."

"Of course not," Mom cooed. "You are our son, and you were a child when we died. None of that was your fault. Please, Grim, don't blame yourself."

I'd lived with this burden my whole life. My sister had even blamed me for our parents' deaths. That guilt was part of me.

But when I looked into their eyes, their shining, beaming eyes, I realized that I had been wrong. That the burden I'd carried could've been eased years ago if I'd just forgiven myself. Because my parents didn't blame me. There was nothing for me but love in their eyes.

"I've blamed myself," I admitted.

"We know." Mom took my hand. For being dead, it was surprisingly warm. "And we don't want you to anymore. There is no one to blame except for the creature who did the deed. Do you understand?"

For the first time since I could remember, I let go of the anger and the blame. The burden had been lifted, and I felt... relieved.

Peace. It was a strange feeling to not be worried and weighed down with guilt. Yet at the same time, this wasn't right.

"There's still more I have to do," I explained. "I've left people, people who need me."

My mother smiled. "Paige. We like her."

My heart, even though I knew that I didn't have one in this ethereal body, pattered against ribs I didn't have, either.

"You have a choice," my father said.

I could stay, or I could return. I could be with my parents and not have pain, worries or anxieties. Or I could return to earth, be with Paige and live the rest of my life, possibly with Carrington Dorn looking over my shoulder, waiting for me to screw up so that he could throw me in prison.

"I know what I want to do," I said.

AND THEN I WAS FALLING, plummeting from the sky and down into my body. I was a bird sailing through the air, and the next thing I knew, I was looking at Paige.

She was sobbing and holding me.

I reached up and touched her cheek. With *my* hand. One that belonged to me, not one that was withered. "Don't cry."

She jumped back; her jaw fell in surprise. Confusion fluttered over her face before realization hit her.

"You're alive! Are you okay?" She didn't wait for an answer before she was hugging me to her, pressing her lips to mine, kissing me hard and fast like she was afraid that I'd slip through her fingers again.

A laugh ripped from my throat. "I'm fine. Better than I've ever been."

She rubbed her thumbs over my cheeks, staring at me with love brimming in her eyes. "Oh! I have to tell Matt!" She turned her head and yelled, "Grim's alive!"

"Help me up."

Very slowly I rose to my feet, inspecting my body on the way. I was completely healed. The puncture wound in my chest was sealed as if it had never existed to begin with.

Matt spotted me and left Carrington Dorn, who had a

THE WITHERING STORM

team of wizards and witches with him, who were currently putting magical shackles on Horatio Crooks and Drea.

My friend pulled me into a bear hug, which elicited a grunt from me. "You know what your problem is, Grim? You don't man-hug enough."

I tipped my head back and laughed, hugging him tighter. When he released me, Matt stepped back and eyed me up and down. "How? You were dead, my friend. Stone-cold dead."

It sounded outlandish even to me, but I managed to get out, "I saw my parents. They offered me a choice, and I took it."

"To be with me?" Matt asked hopefully.

I glared at him.

He lifted his hands in surrender. "I knew it was too much to ask. I was pushing my limit at a hug."

"You saw your parents?" Paige asked. When I nodded, her hands flew to her mouth. "I can't believe it."

My gaze dropped to the ground. It was difficult to admit this, even to those I was closest to. "They told me to let go of the guilt that I've been hanging on to over their deaths. I couldn't have stopped them from dying. They said—they told me to forgive myself."

Her face brightened. "And you are? At least working on that?"

One side of my mouth ticked up in a smile. "I'm working on it the best that I can."

"That's the most that any of us can ask." She rubbed a hand over my shoulder. "I'm just so…I can't believe you're here. You were dead. Gone."

She burst into tears, and I pulled her tight to me.

Matt nodded toward Carrington, silently saying that he was walking off to speak to the wizard, and he gave us some privacy.

She sobbed in my arms for a couple of minutes until she

pulled away and rubbed tears from her cheeks with the heels of her hands. "It's so much to take in. You were one of them, and then you fought, and then you…"

"Died. I died. You can say it." She ripped her gaze from me and gulped down a sob. I dropped my head until we were eye level, and I took her by the shoulders. "Paige, I would never leave you, not if I could help it. Look—death couldn't even keep us apart. It tried and it failed. There are times to be sad, but this isn't one of them. But I know it's a shock. Come. Let's get you something warm to drink."

"I'm never going back inside that house again."

I couldn't blame her there. "Then let me take you to the wizards and witches. They'll have something."

They did. Dorn's crew had an entire cupboard of warm drinks and blankets that they'd brought. I deposited Paige with a witch who had a warm smile, brown hair twisted high on her head, and a fussy, rumpled, just cozy enough look to put Paige's nerves at ease.

After that I approached Dorn.

"Heard you died, Grim," came his salty greeting.

"You know me—I can't stay dead. It'll take a lot more than a withering to kill me."

A ghost of a smile covered his face before he squashed it down. "So Horatio Crooks has some secrets, I hear."

"He has a lot of them. Would you like to see?"

"Do you need to rest first?"

"No. Crooks's secrets need to be revealed, and he needs to go to prison for what he's done."

As we walked toward the house, Dorn glanced up. "You know, I was always a Horatio Crooks fan when I was a kid. I still watch—er, watched him sometimes. But as soon as he had you, I knew something wasn't right."

"What do you mean?"

We'd reached the door, and Dorn stopped, shook his head

of light blond hair. "I don't know, there was just something off about the whole thing. No one's ever saved anyone from a withering before, and the fact that Horatio Crooks seemed to know how rang false with me."

"It was false. He spelled me to think that I was being healed, but his real plan was to keep me as part of his collection."

"How was he going to do that?"

I shook my head. "I think he expected me to transform alone, but when the witherings showed up, it was a surprise, even to him, and it's what eventually cost him everything."

Dorn dropped his head. "And the daughter?"

I shook my head. "I'm sure Matt told you that she's a werewolf."

"One that can change at will? Must be nice to have powers like that."

I watched as Drea was escorted rather forcefully through a portal. "But those powers still couldn't keep the beast out. She was stalking a boy in town and would've eventually killed him if she'd been allowed to keep roaming."

"And Horatio didn't do anything about it?"

"He enabled her," I said darkly.

Dorn hissed. "These people think they're untouchable. Everyone can be brought down. All it takes is the right person to do it. Speaking of, you're lucky you died or else you'd be in shackles, too."

I barked a laugh. "Who would've thought Carrington Dorn would make me laugh."

He smirked. "Better laughing than crying."

I grunted. "Let me show you what Horatio's been up to all these years. I'm afraid you're not going to like it."

Dorn pulled out a pair of black gloves and slid them on. "Let's see what he's got."

27

In the end Dorn and his crew packed up all the creatures and promised to relocate many of them to an animal sanctuary, where they would not only be cared for, but they'd be watched so that they couldn't harm anyone.

It was the best ending that anyone could've hoped for other than Horatio.

As for the star, he pleaded *not guilty* to every charge brought against him, but it didn't matter. The judge gave him the maximum sentence of life in prison.

Drea, who was more a victim of her condition, received a lighter sentence, but she still didn't get off scot-free. She got twenty years.

Horatio's audience may have suffered some of the worst abuses. They were witness to witherings being destroyed and one created. It was them, in fact, and not Matt, who had contacted the authorities. It's how Dorn and his people had arrived so quickly.

And as for me...

"Coffee's on," Shelby called from the kitchen.

"Be there in a second."

THE WITHERING STORM

I walked through the old house, bricks chattering at me, through the French doors that led onto the back deck. I watched as early morning sunlight slowly bled across the sky and a new day began.

As soon as Horatio and Drea were taken into custody, Matt had magicked us back to my sister's house, where I gave Uncle Geezer a good scolding for pairing me up with Horatio.

"My dear boy, I never expected it to go the way it did," he'd assured me.

It was true, so I couldn't hold that against my uncle. He'd only done what he thought was best by bringing Horatio into the fold.

"Morning, sunshine."

I turn around to find Paige grinning at me. She sauntered up and leaned her arms against the railing, pressing her body into mine.

"You look good for someone who died yesterday."

I dropped my head and chuckled. "I feel good for someone who died." She nodded, keeping her gaze trained on the sunrise. "And what about you?"

"Me? Oh, I didn't die."

"I mean, how are you?"

"Well, knowing that you're cured makes me feel pretty amazing. It's the best Christmas, birthday, any-day present I ever could've received."

"You and me both."

I leaned in and brushed my lips to hers. She tasted like mint, smelled of soap, and I wanted to devour her.

"So what do we do now?" she asked.

I hooked my arm around her and pulled her so close that there were no gaps between us. "Now we go home and we forget all about monsters and hunting and just be together."

Never in my life had I wanted to stop hunting, but I'd spent

AMY BOYLES

the last month thinking that I was dying. Well, I had been. Because of that, I'd pushed Paige away, but no more.

Now all I wanted to do was go home, take her with me, lock the door and stay inside for weeks. I was still a hunter and would always be one, but for right now the most important thing to me was her and making sure that she knew it.

She peered up at me from underneath a thick wall of lashes. "Are you sure that's what you want?"

"I'm more sure of that than anything else."

A scraping sound came from the door, and out ran Savage, wings spread as if he was about to fly. My dog leaped, and I caught him in my arms.

As he bathed my face with his tongue, I smiled and held him out. "I saw you yesterday, Savage."

"He missed you," Paige mused.

Right behind Savage trotted Footie, the magicked footstool. Footie plodded over to Paige, who gave the object a swift pat.

"There. Now you're not left out," she mused.

I put Savage down as Matt and Shelby came out, each of them holding two cups of coffee.

"Black," he said, offering me a cup. "Just like I thought your heart was when we first met."

I grunted. "At least you're honest."

"To be fair, I thought your heart was black, too," Paige said.

"I've always thought that," Shelby said with a wink. She gave Paige a cup and sipped from the mug in her hand. "Beautiful morning."

"It sure is," Matt said, coyly watching her.

"Geezer still asleep?" I asked.

"Yeah. He'll be up in a bit. I know he's glad that you're home, Grim. I am, too."

"Words I never thought that I'd hear my sister say."

She smirked, but a twinkle filled her eyes. After we'd

THE WITHERING STORM

returned, I pulled her aside and told her about seeing our parents. She cried, of course. But was happy that they were at peace.

Matt inhaled deeply. "So Grim, what's next for you? You going monster hunting?"

My gaze zeroed in on Paige. "I'm taking a break from hunting for a while."

"Why, and I was just about to say, you know what your problem is? You don't take enough vacations. Seems like you're finally getting it."

I smiled. "I am. I'm taking Paige and going home. There's an ex-withering trapped in a book that needs to be released. He committed murder, so will still be going to prison, but as a human. What about you? You're a free man, not cursed and not forced to help me. Where is life going to take you?"

Matt smiled bashfully at Shelby, and she grinned back. "I think I'm going to stick around here for a bit. See what lady luck throws my way."

I had a feeling that a spring wedding was on the horizon. I reached out and shook his hand. "Wherever life takes you, remember that you've got a lifelong friend in me."

"Will do."

We were quiet for a moment until Shelby broke the silence. "Breakfast?"

"Yes," I told them. "I'm starving."

In all, we stayed a couple more days with my sister. It'd be a lie to say that I was one hundred percent the person I was before I allowed the withering to overtake me. I wasn't the same. There was still a smudge of darkness lurking in my heart, but it was easy to recognize and push aside, keeping it at bay.

Finally it was time to leave. The morning was beautiful as I loaded up the last of our bags in my car. Paige came up behind me and rubbed a hand down my back. "I'm going to leave my car here. See if Matt and Shelby can bring it in a month when they come to visit."

I turned around and pulled her into a hug. "Sounds like a plan. Are you ready?"

She cocked her head, her eyes searching mine, silently asking if I was truly okay. "That depends. Are you?"

"I'm ready to put all of this behind us."

"Then let's go home."

She slid her hands into mine, and I kissed her, long and deep.

Though the darkness would never truly be banished from my heart, Paige would be by my side, and she was enough light to remind me of who I really was.

"Yes," I said, pressing my lips to her, "let's go home."

THANK you for reading A WITHERING STORM. Stay up to date on all my releases and sales by signing up for my newsletter HERE.

ALSO BY AMY BOYLES

OTHER SERIES

SEVEN WITCHES FOR SEVEN SUITORS (Romance)

HOW TO FAKE IT WITH A FAE

A MAGICAL RENOVATION MYSERY

WITCHER UPPER

RENOVATION SPELL

DEMOLITION PREMONITION

WITCHER UPPER CHRISTMAS

BARN BEWITCHMENT

SHIPLAP AND SPELL HUNTING

MUDROOM MYSTIC

WITCH IT OR LIST IT

PANTRY PRANKSTER

HOME TOWN MAGIC

WITCH APPEAL

WHITE MAGIC AND WARDROBES

RESTORATION RUNES

LOST SOUTHERN MAGIC

(Takes place following the events of Southern Magic Wedding. This
is a Sweet Tea Witches, Southern Belles and Spells, Southern Ghost
Wrangles and Bless Your Witch Crossover)

THE GOLD TOUCH THAT WENT CATTYWAMPUS

THE YELLOW-BELLIED SCAREDY CAT

A MESS OF SIRENS

KNEE-HIGH TO A THIEF

BELLES AND SPELLS MATCHMAKER MYSTERY

DEADLY SPELLS AND A SOUTHERN BELLE

CURSED BRIDES AND ALIBIS

MAGICAL DAMES AND DATING GAMES

SOME PIG AND A MUMMY DIG

SWEET TEA WITCH MYSTERIES

SOUTHERN MAGIC

SOUTHERN SPELLS

SOUTHERN MYTHS

SOUTHERN SORCERY

SOUTHERN CURSES

SOUTHERN KARMA

SOUTHERN MAGIC THANKSGIVING

SOUTHERN MAGIC CHRISTMAS

SOUTHERN POTIONS

SOUTHERN FORTUNES

SOUTHERN HAUNTINGS

SOUTHERN WANDS

SOUTHERN CONJURING

SOUTHERN WISHES

SOUTHERN DREAMS

SOUTHERN MAGIC WEDDING

SOUTHERN OMENS

SOUTHERN JINXED

SOUTHERN BEGINNINGS

SOUTHERN MYSTICS

SOUTHERN CAULDRONS

SOUTHERN HOLIDAY

SOUTHERN ENCHANTED

SOUTHERN TRAPPINGS

THE ACCIDENTAL MEDIUM

WITCH'S BLOCK

POISONED PROSE

SPELL, DON'T TELL

SOUTHERN GHOST WRANGLER MYSTERIES

SOUL FOOD SPIRITS

HONEYSUCKLE HAUNTING

THE GHOST WHO ATE GRITS (Crossover with Pepper and Axel
from Sweet Tea Witches)

BACKWOODS BANSHEE

MISTLETOE AND SPIRITS

BLESS YOUR WITCH SERIES

SCARED WITCHLESS

KISS MY WITCH

QUEEN WITCH

QUIT YOUR WITCHIN'

FOR WITCH'S SAKE

DON'T GIVE A WITCH

WITCH MY GRITS

FRIED GREEN WITCH

SOUTHERN WITCHING

Y'ALL WITCHES

HOLD YOUR WITCHES

SOUTHERN SINGLE MOM PARANORMAL MYSTERIES
The Witch's Handbook to Hunting Vampires
The Witch's Handbook to Catching Werewolves
The Witch's Handbook to Trapping Demons

ABOUT THE AUTHOR

Hey, I'm Amy,

I write books for folks who crave laugh-out-loud paranormal romance and cozy mysteries. I've got a Pharm D and a BA in Creative Writing.

And when I'm not writing, I can be found reading or binge-watching a K-drama. If you have any suggestions on good K-dramas, I will take them!

If you want to reach out to me—and I love to hear from readers—you can email me at amy@amyboyles.com

Happy reading!